W9-CBP-683

KING of the MOUND

My Summer with Satchel Paige

WES TOOKE

Simon & Schuster Books for Young Readers
New York London Toronto Sydney New Delhi

Also by Wes Tooke

Lucky

SIMON & SCHUSTER BOOKS FOR YOUNG READERS
An imprint of Simon & Schuster Children's Publishing Division
1230 Avenue of the Americas, New York, New York 10020
This book is a work of fiction. Any references to historical events, real people,
or real locales are used fictitiously. Other names, characters, places, and incidents are products
of the author's imagination, and any resemblance to actual events or locales or persons,
living or dead, is entirely coincidental.

For information about special discounts for bulk purchases, please contact Simon & Schuster
Special Sales at 1-866-506-1949 or business@simonandschuster.com.
The Simon & Schuster Speakers Bureau can bring authors to your live event.
For more information or to book an event, contact the Simon & Schuster Speakers Bureau
at 1-866-248-3049 or visit our website at www.simonspeakers.com.
Book design by Krista Vossen
The text for this book is set in Melior.
Manufactured in the United States of America
0112 FFG
2 4 6 8 10 9 7 5 3 1
Library of Congress Cataloging-in-Publication Data
Tooke, Wes.
King of the Mound: My Summer with Satchel Paige / Wes Tooke. — 1st ed.
p. cm.
Summary: Twelve-year-old Nick loves baseball so after a year in the hospital fighting polio and with
a brace on one leg, Nick takes a job with the team for which his father is catcher and gets to see the
great pitcher, Satchel Paige, play during the 1935 season. Includes historical notes.
ISBN 978-1-4424-3346-5 (hardcover)
[1. Baseball—Fiction. 2. People with disabilities—Fiction. 3. Fathers and sons—Fiction. 4. Paige,
Satchel, 1906-1982—Fiction. 5. African Americans—Fiction. 6. Poliomyelitis—Fiction. 7. Bismarck
(N.D.)—Fiction.] I. Title.
PZ7.T638Her 2012
[Fic]—dc22
2011012740
ISBN 978-1-4424-3348-9 (eBook)

FIRST
EDITION

For my wife

Acknowledgments

I am grateful to Courtney Bongiolatti and Simon & Schuster for supporting this project and to Dan Lazar at Writers House for his diligence. I am also grossly indebted to the work of numerous writers and historians, especially William Price Fox, who conducted a fabulous series of interviews with Satchel recorded in *Satchel Paige's America*, and an essay by Travis Larsen entitled "Satchel Paige and Hap Dumont: The Dynamic Duo of the National Baseball Congress Tournament." Several of Fox's stories from his interviews with Satchel—including a few quotes—are dramatized in this book.

CHAPTER ONE

TOP of the FIRST

Nick stared at the strike zone and took a deep breath. That was something his dad had taught him; he said it relaxed your shoulders and cleared your head. As soon as Nick's lungs were empty, he began his windup, the movements as smooth and natural as the breath he had just taken, until—

SMACK! The rubber ball nailed the center of the chalk square on the wall, skipped neatly on the polished linoleum, and landed next to Nick in the hospital bed.

"Twenty-nine," Nick said to himself.

He picked up the ball, focused on the chalk target again, and took another breath. But before he could begin his windup, Dr. Miller appeared in the door.

"Are you wearing out my wall again?" Dr. Miller asked. He kept a straight face, but Nick knew he was joking—Dr. Miller was the only adult in the whole hospital who wasn't afraid to laugh.

"I'm trying to break my record before I leave," Nick said.

"What's your record?"

Nick pointed at the chalk square. "Inside the strike zone eighty-seven times in a row."

Dr. Miller raised an eyebrow. "Eighty-seven is a whole lot."

"I guess," Nick said. "But not as many as eighty-eight."

This time Dr. Miller did smile. "You keep that attitude and you're going to be fine. Are you ready to go?"

Nick felt his heart speed up—the same nervous feeling he used to get when there was a man on third base and nobody out. "He's here?"

"Waiting downstairs." Dr. Miller glanced at Nick's duffel bag, which was lying next to the door. "You tighten up your brace and I'll get the bag."

"I'll take the bag," Nick said. "He won't like it if I'm not carrying my own bag."

Nick could tell that Dr. Miller was staring at him, but he kept his eyes locked on the metal bar at the foot of his bed. He hated the look that doctors and nurses would sometimes get—like they felt sorry for you but didn't know what to say. Nick didn't want pity. Maybe his left leg didn't work the way it was supposed to, but most of the kids who came through the ward had worse problems. Polio was a terrifying disease. In mild cases you would get symptoms similar to the flu, but if you were sick enough to get transferred to this hospital, it meant you had nerve damage, which often meant paralysis. Some of the kids on the ward couldn't walk at all—or even sit up in bed. And the very sickest ones couldn't breathe for themselves and had to be stuck in a terrifying machine called an iron lung.

"Fine," Dr. Miller said after a long pause. "But let's get you in that brace."

The brace was made of iron with two creaky hinges and thick leather straps. It stretched from the top of Nick's thigh to just above his ankle, and when he wore it for more than a few hours, it would chafe and leave big red swaths on his skin. But at least he could limp around with the brace, which was certainly better than being a prisoner to a wheelchair.

It took a few minutes to fasten the buckles, and when they were finally done, Nick slung the bag over his shoulder and limped down the hall, Dr. Miller next to him.

"You must be excited to see your friends," Dr. Miller said as they entered the elevator.

Nick shrugged. "It's been a year. They probably forgot about me."

"I doubt that. You're a pretty memorable kid."

Nick ignored the comment because he had other stuff on his mind. Over the past year Nick had imagined this moment a thousand times, but it still felt weird to be leaving the ward. On some level Nick had never really believed that his father would actually come—the only time he'd visited the hospital was for an hour at Christmas—so Nick hadn't even bothered to say good-bye to the other kids. But Nick knew they'd understand. People came and went on the polio ward, which was why nobody ever got too attached.

When the elevator doors finally opened, Nick immediately saw the familiar face across the stark lobby. His father always looked out of place anywhere but behind home plate. He was stocky and bowlegged, with deep lines around his dark eyes from spending years squinting in the sun. Their landlord in Bismarck used to joke that the stork must have gotten lost the day he delivered Nick because he and his father were like opposites—Nick was tall and thin for his age, with sandy blond hair and blue eyes. Supposedly he looked like his mother, but his father didn't have any old pictures so Nick didn't know for sure.

His father noticed them emerge from the elevator, and he trudged across the lobby, his worn felt hat in his calloused hand. He gave Nick a long look and then turned to Dr. Miller.

"Is that brace permanent?" he asked.

Dr. Miller ignored the question and stuck out his hand. "I'm Dr. Miller," he said. "You've got a fine son."

Nick's father reddened as they shook hands. "Thanks, doc. And I surely appreciate you looking after him. It's just . . ." His voice trailed off, his eyes locked on the brace, and Nick suddenly wished he were wearing pants instead of shorts.

"Nick's doing great," Dr. Miller said. "But I'd be wary of giving you a specific prognosis."

"Can he pitch? Can he play ball?"

"Once again, I don't want to make any predictions. But I think a more realistic goal is for Nick to be able to walk without a brace."

"So he's a cripple."

Dr. Miller pursed his lips. "That's not a word we like to use around here."

They were quiet for a long moment. Nick stared at his feet, trying to keep the shock from his face. Had his father really just called him that word? *Cripple?* Just as he felt like he might burst, Nick felt a hand on his shoulder. It was Dr. Miller.

"Good luck, Nick," he said. "We'll miss you."

"I'll miss you too," Nick said.

As Nick followed his father into the parking lot, he realized that it wasn't exactly the truth and wasn't exactly a lie. He wouldn't miss the sharp, antiseptic smell of the ward or the chatter of the nurses early in the morning or that horrible, lonely feeling you got just before you fell asleep. But nobody in the hospital had ever called him a *cripple*. Why would his father say something like that? Unlike most of the kids in the ward, Nick could wash himself and eat normally and even walk. And, yeah, maybe he had to wear a brace, but did that mean he was permanently broken? Was that really what people outside the hospital would think about him?

His father stopped in front of a strange-looking brown Chrysler and waited impatiently for Nick to catch up. The car was long with an enormous hood and hardly any straight lines.

"You got a car?" Nick asked.

"Mr. Churchill lent it to me."

"It's nice," Nick said, trying to be polite.

His father rolled his eyes. "Are you crazy? That newfangled body looks like a squashed cow patty. And those idiots in Detroit built it so badly that the engine falls out whenever it hits eighty."

"Well, I like the color," Nick said.

His father grunted, grabbed the bag from Nick's shoulder, and tossed it in the backseat. He started around the car and then paused and glanced at Nick.

"Can you get in by yourself or do I have to help you?" he asked.

"I can do it," Nick said.

❋   ❋   ❋

It was a long drive back to Bismarck—almost five hundred miles. They headed north to Minneapolis, northwest to Fargo, and then due west across the rolling plain. The journey was brutal in the winter when the arctic wind was whipping snow across the road, but now, in early June, they cruised along with the windows cracked to let the sweet summer breeze into the car.

As they drove, Nick couldn't help thinking about the last time he'd been on these roads. Polio had ambushed him. One morning in late May he woke up with a fever and a stiff neck, and the moment the doctor heard his symptoms he was whisked into quarantine at the local hospital in Bismarck. At first Nick hadn't been worried—other kids in his neighborhood had gotten polio and been okay. But the second morning he felt pins and needles in his legs, and he knew he was in trouble because the doctors kept whispering in the hall outside his room. By the time they put him in a truck to drive him to the Mayo Clinic, Nick had been fading in and out of consciousness, and all he really remembered about the journey was his father's stone expression and the soothing feeling of the nurse dabbing his forehead with a cold washcloth.

But this time there was no nurse and no washcloth, and Nick spent most of the long drive staring out the window at the passing plains, bored. They had to stop three times for gas and oil, and once for sandwiches, and it was almost midnight by the time the car was finally rolling down Main Street. They had barely spoken two words since they left the hospital, but as they caught a glimpse of the stadium, Nick felt that old familiar rush of excitement and couldn't contain himself.

"How's the team this year?" he asked.

"Best in the Dakotas," his father said. "Maybe the best semipro club in the Midwest. Just depends how many more of those colored boys Mr. Churchill signs up."

"Who have you got?"

"Satch, supposedly. And Red and Barney Morris. And there's rumors about Double Duty Radcliffe."

Nick tried to keep the excitement out of his voice. "Satch is coming back?"

"I'll believe it when I see it," his father said.

Nick wanted to ask more questions, but he knew from his father's tone that any further attempts at conversation would be answered with silence. It seemed impossible to believe that Satchel Paige might actually return to Bismarck. Of course, Nick never would have guessed that one of the greatest living pitchers would come to Bismarck in the first place, but that was only because Satch was black and the majors wouldn't let black players in the league.

And so two years earlier—the fall of 1933—Mr. Churchill, the team's owner, had convinced Satch to pitch the last month of the season for Bismarck. He was nothing short of amazing as he won six of his seven starts and averaged almost fifteen strikeouts a game. Nick's father had caught four of those games, and Nick, who was ten at the time, had sat in the first row of the stands and watched as Satch's magical arm bewildered helpless batters. Satch had promised to return the following season, and the team had even rebuilt the stadium to handle the expected crowd. In fact, that had been one of the things that Nick dreaded most when he went into the hospital—the idea that Satch might be pitching in Bismarck while he was trapped in a ward five hundred miles away had been too painful to contemplate.

But Satch never showed up, not even after Mr. Churchill threatened to have policemen drag him back to Bismarck to fulfill his contract. Nick had followed the story in the papers—the rumor had been that another team was paying Satch more money—and in the wake of that nasty fight, Nick had assumed that North Dakota had seen the last of the great Satchel Paige. He was *very* glad to be wrong.

"We're here," his father said, interrupting Nick's thoughts.

The car had pulled up outside a dilapidated house on the outskirts of town. Nick stared at the peeling paint and weathered door.

"Why did you move out of Mr. Powell's place?" he asked.

"Rent went up," his father said. "Let's go."

Nick grabbed his duffel from the backseat and then followed his father down a gravel path that led to a little cabin behind the main house. The moon was bright, but Nick still stumbled as he climbed up the stairs to the sagging porch. His father caught him by the shoulder and then roughly grabbed the bag.

"Quiet," he said. "If you wake Mrs. Landry, I'm going to hear about it in the morning."

As they entered the cabin, his father flipped a switch next to the door and a naked bulb flickered to life. The inside was just one tiny room with a bed, a sink, a chair, and a small cot. Nick's father tossed the duffel in the corner and then began stripping off his clothes while Nick settled on the cot and struggled to undo the leather straps on his brace.

"You're working for Mr. Churchill this summer," Nick's father said when he was wearing just a T-shirt and his oil-stained pants. "He's been real nice paying for the hospital and letting me borrow the car and everything, so you're going to give him a hand. That's the deal."

"At the dealership or with the team?" Nick asked.

"Whatever he wants." Nick's father glanced at his brace again. "Whatever you can actually do. Understand?"

"Yes, sir."

His father flipped off the light and then grunted as he settled into bed. Nick kept fumbling with the straps of his brace in the dark—he would never be able to fall asleep with that thing clamped to his leg.

"Good night, Dad," he said after a minute.

Silence. Nick kept working on the straps, and when the last one was finally undone, he lay down on the lumpy cot and pulled the rough wool blanket over his clothes.

He was back.

CHAPTER TWO

BOTTOM *of the* FIRST

Nick awoke to a scratchy sound. His father was shaving—staring into a tiny mirror above the sink as he intently concentrated on the sharp blade—but he stopped and turned around when Nick swung his legs off the cot.

"I'm going to the dealership," he said. "I'll come get you if Mr. Churchill needs anything."

"You want me to wait here all day?" Nick asked.

"Clean up the room. And there are weeds that need pulling in the yard."

Nick's bladder felt like a balloon about to burst, and he glanced around the tiny cabin. "Where's the bathroom?"

"Outhouse." His father flicked his head at the door. "Follow the trail behind the cabin."

Nick strapped on his brace, but this time he covered it with a pair of pants. When he was dressed, he went outside. The trail led through a small stand of birch trees to a wood outhouse with a moon cut in the door for ventilation.

Nick braced himself before he stepped inside—the outhouse at his father's previous cabin had smelled like a medieval sewer—but this one must have been relatively new because it still had the faint scent of pine.

By the time Nick returned to the cabin, his father and the car were gone, but he had left half a loaf of bread and a hunk of cheese sitting on the cot. Nick wolfed down his breakfast and then made the beds, swept the room, and unpacked his duffel into a battered chest of drawers. When he was finished, he returned to the yard. The sun was higher now and the morning was getting hot, so he stripped down to his T-shirt before settling onto his knees and tearing handfuls of weeds away from the base of the cabin.

Nick had been working for only a few minutes when he heard a door slam behind him. He glanced back at the main house and saw a girl walking toward him across the patchy lawn. She was wearing a gray dress patched with mismatched fabric, and worn leather shoes.

"Hey, Nick," she said.

Nick struggled to his feet, wondering how she knew his name. She was about his age, with long brown hair, dark eyes, and skin as pale as the women in the movies. "Hey," Nick said after an awkward pause.

The girl was staring at him, a funny smile on her face. "You don't recognize me?" Nick shook his head. "I'm Emma Landry. I was a year behind you in school, remember?"

The name sparked a memory in Nick's head of a skinny kid with big eyes, but the memory had almost nothing in common with the girl standing in front of him. "You're . . . bigger," Nick finally said.

Emma shrugged. "You've been gone a long time."

Nick felt a pang in his stomach. It was true—he had been gone a long time. And during the year he had been trapped in the hospital, life in Bismarck had kept moving. Kids had grown, friendships had been made and lost, things had *changed*.

"Are you okay?" Emma asked. She was still staring at him. "You look sad."

"I'm fine."

"It's going to be a good day. Aren't you excited to see Satch?"

Nick cocked his head, confused. "What do you mean?"

"He arrived last night. They're having a ceremony at the ballpark."

"Today?"

"I'm leaving in five minutes."

"Why? Girls don't like baseball."

Emma arched an eyebrow. "That's obviously not true because I'm a girl and I've seen every home game for the last two seasons. Not to mention that I know all sorts of facts. Like the fact that you once struck out nine batters in four innings. Even though you were the youngest pitcher in youth baseball."

Nick felt his face flush. "Sorry," he said after a long moment. "I guess girls can like baseball. I just never knew any who did."

"Well, now you know me. Which is good because we're neighbors." Emma flicked her head at the road. "Want to walk together to the game? If we go now, we might be able to sneak really close to home plate."

"I can't," Nick said.

"What? Why not?"

"My father will kill me if he comes back and I'm not here."

Emma shrugged. "Just leave a note."

"He's not much of a reader."

"You have to go," she said. "It's Satchel Paige. In our town!"

Nick knew she was right. Sure, he was nervous about leaving the house without his dad's permission—and he was even more nervous about the idea of walking all the way to the stadium on his brace, since the hardest he'd pushed his leg in the hospital were short strolls up and down the corridor. But those fears didn't stand a chance against two simple facts: First, Nick hadn't seen any real baseball in more than a year, and second, one of the best pitchers in the world was about to be standing on a mound less than a mile from his house.

"Fine," Nick said. "But I can't stay long."

The baseball stadium was on the south side of Bismarck, and Emma and Nick took the shortest route, which was a dirt lane that ran along the outskirts of town. When Mr. Churchill signed Nick's dad to play catcher and they first came to Bismarck, the town had been an island of houses amid a sea of corn and wheat, but a ferocious series of windstorms had blown away the topsoil, and now the fields were bare and dusty. You could always tell the farmers from the townspeople because the farmers had a lost, desperate look in their eyes. That was why Nick's father had kept playing with a broken bone in his hand two seasons earlier. As he said at the time: "These people ain't got nothing. So the least we can do is give them some baseball."

By the time the stadium finally appeared behind a row of poorly constructed aluminum shacks, Nick's leg was aching and one of the straps on his brace was cutting into his thigh like a saw. Nick stared at the new grandstand and the row of wooden bleachers that had risen in right field.

"It looks like a real stadium now," he said.

"Yeah," Emma said. "And maybe it will actually be full since Satch is here."

As they approached the main gate, Nick noticed a man selling tickets and a sign that read SEE THE RETURN OF THE LEGEND. JUST FIVE CENTS!

"I don't have any money," Nick said, a sinking feeling in his stomach.

"We don't need money," Emma said. "Follow me."

She led him down the third base side of the stadium until they were a hundred yards away from the main gate, and then she reached down and grabbed the bottom of the chain-link fence.

"Roll," she said as she yanked the wire upward.

Nick gave her a glance and then dropped to the ground. The fence scratched his arm as he rolled, but then he was inside. As he pushed himself to his feet, Emma popped up next to him, a devilish grin on her face.

"It's the bargain entrance," she said.

"Hey!" a voice shouted from the main gate. "Get over here!"

Emma grabbed Nick's hand and pulled him toward the field. "Don't look back," she said. "Hurry!"

Nick did his best to keep up with her, half hopping on his stupid brace as they ran around the corner of the grandstand.

He thought they were going to cut up into the crowd, but instead she ducked through a small hole and suddenly they were lost amid a maze of iron latticework under the stands. It smelled like fresh mud and stale beer, and the wood above them creaked as people moved toward their seats. Nick glanced at Emma. She was staring at his bad leg.

"Is that from polio?" she asked. He nodded. "Does it hurt?"

"Not really."

"Can you pitch?"

Nick shook his head. "I'd probably fall over on the mound."

"Have you tried?"

"Nope."

"Well, you won't know until you try."

Nick thought that was pretty obvious—and didn't really want to talk about what he could or could not do—so he just grunted and crept toward the front of the grandstand. There was a little gap between the stairs that ran up between the sections, and whenever the aisle cleared, he could get a look at the field. In dead center was a parking lot where people could watch the game from their cars—the first time Satch pitched, desperate fans had stood on roofs and hoods to catch a glimpse. To the right of the parking lot stretched the new bleachers, mostly covered with families, and the new grandstand circled the infield. It was at least thirty rows high and packed with fans.

"It's full," Nick said.

"The stadium seats almost five thousand now," Emma said. "Half the people in Bismarck can fit in here."

Nick shook his head. "Mr. Churchill sure must have been mad when Satch didn't show up."

"I heard he beat up a brand-new car," she said. "Smashed the windshield and everything."

"I wonder why he let Satch come back."

Emma shrugged. "Because he can pitch."

Nick knew Emma was right. His father claimed that a star pitcher would always have a job no matter how crazy he was. "Great players live their lives by different rules," his father had said more than once. "At least until they can't play anymore. And then people dump them twice as fast because they never could stand to be around them."

The grandstand above Nick suddenly rumbled as hundreds of people pushed themselves to their feet. A gate had opened in center field, and a silver convertible was slowly driving toward the pitcher's mound, Mr. Churchill and Satch perched in the backseat. Satch was wearing the team uniform—a white jersey with "Bismarck" printed across the chest in bold letters—and waving at the crowd, a bemused half smile on his face. Mr. Churchill was significantly shorter than Satch but at least three times as wide. He had once been a good baseball player, but those days were long gone, and according to Nick's father he weighed almost three hundred pounds. In a town of skinny, hardscrabble people he stood out like an elephant in a herd of cattle. Today he was wearing a white linen suit that draped over his massive body like a tent, and he was pointing and winking at people in the crowd as the car slowed to a stop near second base.

"I can't see," Emma said. "Let's go up in the stands."

"What about the guard?"

"He won't be looking for us. Not with Satch on the mound."

Emma turned and slipped through the hole in the grand-stand. Nick followed her, and a moment later they found a spot amid a family in the front row. Satch and Mr. Churchill had gotten out of the convertible, and Mr. Churchill was holding a megaphone to his mouth.

"Behold the return of the great Satchel Paige!" he bellowed. His voice was as loud as a steam engine. "A legend who needs no introduction . . . a man who dazzled us with his talents two summers ago. Inventor and master of pitches too numerous to name, including the Bat Dodger, Midnight Creeper, Four-Day Rider, Nothin' Ball, and infamous Rising Tom!"

While Mr. Churchill was shouting, a black man in a dark suit emerged from the dugout and strolled to home plate.

"I think that's Double Duty," Emma whispered.

Nick craned his neck to see. Double Duty Radcliffe was one of the most versatile players in baseball: He had earned his nickname during the 1932 Negro League World Series when he caught a shutout from Satch in the first game and then threw a shutout in the second. He was short and squat and had a reputation for making jokes during games—Nick's father had said that when Double Duty caught, he some-times wore a chest protector with the words "Thou Shalt Not Steal" written across the front.

Nick glanced back at Satch, who was twirling a ball in his hands on the mound, and Nick knew he was about to see something special. For Satch's first appearance two years earlier, Mr. Churchill had put a book of matches atop a stick at home plate, and Satch had hit the matchbook thirteen times out of twenty. But Nick knew enough about show-manship to understand that they couldn't do the same thing again—this time the stunt had to be bigger. Better.

Double Duty dug into the batter's box as if he were going to hit, but then he withdrew a pack of cigarettes and a book of matches from his suit pocket. A moment later a lit cigarette was dangling from his lips. Satch stared in at home plate as if waiting for the sign, his long arms dangling loosely by his sides and his intense brown eyes narrowed into menacing slits.

"Play ball!" Mr. Churchill shouted.

Satch began his windup, his leg rising almost as high as his ear, and then whipped his body toward home plate. Double Duty stood motionless as the white streak rocketed toward his face. People in the crowd screamed. Nick felt Emma grab his arm—

And then the ball clipped the cigarette and slammed into the bottom of the backstop. Double Duty casually leaned over and picked up the cigarette from the ground.

"It gone out!" he loudly announced.

The crowd exploded into wild applause. Nick smiled at Emma, his hands pounding together. When he looked back at the field, Mr. Churchill was pointing at Satch.

"Now show them what they came to see," Mr. Churchill shouted. "Show them the Rising Tom!"

A familiar figure trotted out of the dugout—Nick's father, wearing his uniform and a catching mask. As he settled into position behind home plate, Satch made a show of stretching his arm.

It's not fair, Nick thought. *They shouldn't make him try to catch a Rising Tom when he hasn't seen it for two years. Not in front of a crowd.*

"Does the Rising Tom really rise?" Emma asked, interrupting his thoughts.

Nick shrugged. "That's what they say."

Satch's leg kicked high again, and then the ball was flashing toward home plate, spinning so fast that it was just a blur. Nick's father stabbed upward at the last moment, but the ball nicked off the top of his glove and smashed into the backstop with a sound like a gunshot.

As the crowd erupted into applause again, Satch waved broadly and then started toward the convertible. Nick's father was trudging back to retrieve the ball, his jaw clenched. Nick knew why he was upset—he couldn't stand to be embarrassed. As he leaned over to pick up the ball, his angry eyes scanned the crowd. At the last moment Nick realized what was about to happen, and he tried to duck behind the man next to him. But he was too slow.

They stared at each other for a moment that felt like an hour. And then his father shook his head, an expression on his face that Nick recognized.

He'd been home for less than a day and already he was in trouble.

CHAPTER THREE

TOP *of the* SECOND

Nick sat on his cot and waited for his father to return from the ballpark. It felt like being slow-roasted over a smoldering fire—every minute he got more and more anxious until eventually his brain just shut down and he stared blankly at the floor. Finally his father's boots clumped up the stairs and the door swung open.

"Out," his father said.

Nick glanced up. His father was pointing at the porch, expressionless. Nick pushed himself to his feet and hobbled outside. As he settled onto the rough wood of the porch, a wool blanket landed next to him, and a moment later the door slammed closed. The sun had set and the only light came from a pair of lit windows in the main house. Occasionally a shadow moved behind the curtains—maybe Emma.

Nick had been on the porch for maybe ten or fifteen minutes when he smelled the fire, and a few minutes later he heard the crackle from the frying pan, and then the thick, rich scent of bacon drifted onto the porch. His stomach growled—it felt like there was a tight fist behind his belly button squeezing nothing but air. The temperature was also dropping with each passing moment, and Nick pulled the blanket around his shoulders and lay back on the porch. Was he really going to have to sleep outside?

As the seconds turned into minutes and the sliver of a moon began to move across the sky, Nick felt his anger begin to simmer. It wasn't fair—he had done his chores before he went to the game. Did his father expect him to hide at the house all day? Maybe that was it; maybe he didn't want the other players to know he had a crippled son. But it wasn't Nick's fault that he had gotten polio, and he wasn't going to spend the rest of his life hiding. No matter what his father wanted.

Just as Nick's anger reached its peak, the door swung open and his father loomed over him, a faceless shadow in the dark.

"You're not a little kid anymore," he said, his voice a low growl. "You want to live here and eat my food, then you live under my rules. You do what I say when I say it. Understand?"

"Yes," Nick said quietly.

"Yes, what?"

The anger was a fierce ball of flame high in his chest, and Nick had to swallow hard before he could speak. "Yes, sir."

"Okay," his father said. "Get inside."

The smell of bacon had been coming from a square of fatback, which his father cut in half and then put on two large slices of rye bread. Nick wolfed down his food, and the moment he finished, his father blew out the lamp. For the second time in two nights Nick undid his brace in the dark, and by the time he lay down, his father's resonant snores were echoing around the tiny cabin. Nick had never imagined that he might miss the hospital, but at this moment he felt more isolated lying ten feet away from his father than during all of those lonely nights on the polio ward.

The next morning Nick was sweeping the porch when his father emerged from the cabin, the worn duffel he used to carry his equipment slung over his shoulder.

"Let's go," he said. "I told Mr. Churchill we'd be there at eight."

Nick felt elated as he put away the broom. He didn't know where they were going or what they would be doing, but anything was better than staying at the cabin all day. His father was already walking toward the street, and Nick had to half hop on his good leg to catch him.

"I'll carry your bag," Nick said.

His father gave him a long look. That had been their routine before Nick went to the hospital—he would carry the duffel to the park so his father wouldn't wear down his legs before the game. It had started when Nick was young enough that the bag was practically as big as him, but now . . .

"It's fine," Nick said. "It's not like I'm going to break or something."

After another agonizing moment his father grunted and dropped the bag on the dirt driveway. "Just keep up," he said.

Nick couldn't tell if his father was moving faster than

usual or if he just had longer legs than Emma, but the walk to the ballpark was brutal. His brace was rubbing his skin raw and the strap of the duffel cut into his shoulder and his lower back felt like it had been beaten with a baseball bat. But there was no way he was going to slow down—not after the look his father had given him—so he just gritted his teeth and pretended he was a soldier on a long march. The last hundred paces were pure torture—his shoulder was on fire—and when his father finally stopped next to a little shack near the entrance to the grandstand, Nick gratefully slung the bag to the ground.

"Where's Mr. Churchill?" Nick asked when he got his breath.

His father just pointed down the road. A billowing cloud of dust was moving toward them, and as it got closer Nick realized that it was the same strange-looking brown Chrysler that he and his father had driven back from the hospital. It slowed to a stop in front of the shack, and Mr. Churchill opened the door and rolled himself out of the car. He was wearing a pink shirt with a blue bow tie, black pants, and yellow suspenders.

"Morning, Ben," he said to Nick's father. As his pale blue eyes moved to Nick, the corners of his round mouth turned up in a smile. "Glad to see you up and about," he said. "Feeling better?"

"Yes, sir," Nick said. "Much better."

"That's good. Your pops was real worried about you. Weren't you, Ben?"

"Yup," Nick's father said.

Mr. Churchill smiled again. "Always a big talker." He

came around the car and clapped Nick on the shoulder. "I hear you're going to be my new ace employee this summer. I was thinking you could handle my payroll. Maybe do my taxes. What do you think of that?"

Nick knew it was a joke, but he also knew Mr. Churchill liked it when people played along with him. "I don't know much about taxes," Nick said. "But I'm pretty good at sweeping and cleaning and stuff."

Mr. Churchill threw back his head and laughed, his cheeks rippling like sheets in the wind. Nick didn't know why it was funny, but he also remembered that Mr. Churchill didn't need much of an excuse to laugh.

"I'll bet you're a champion sweeper," Mr. Churchill said when he caught his breath. "But we'll find something more interesting for you to do. At least this first day."

None of the other players had arrived yet, and Nick's father went to the field, where he did his usual morning routine of sit-ups and push-ups, while Nick helped Mr. Churchill carry a cardboard box from the trunk of his convertible into the small shack that served as the team's office. When they were inside, Mr. Churchill tore open the box and then stared inside, shaking his head. Nick peeked around him and saw more than a dozen baseball mitts.

"I don't know what I was thinking," Mr. Churchill said. "I told the Rawlings people I'd get every player on our team to use their stuff, but trying to get a player to switch gloves is like trying to get a cat to swim backstroke."

"It's hard to break in a glove," Nick said.

"That's true, but it's also superstition. Baseball players are afraid of change." Mr. Churchill picked up one of the gloves and gave it a trial squeeze. "But maybe you're right. Maybe if we break in these gloves before we give them to the guys, there's a chance they'll actually wear them. What do you think?"

Nick felt a warm glow in his stomach—he liked that Mr. Churchill had asked for his opinion. "Yeah, that might help," he said.

Mr. Churchill clapped his shoulder. "Then that's your first assignment. Break in these gloves for me."

A moment later Mr. Churchill went out to the field to inspect the grandstand, and Nick's heart sank. Breaking in just one glove was a major undertaking, and there were fifteen gloves in the box. They were all the new Rawlings model with the special deep well pocket, the leather so stiff that in order to fold the mitt around the ball you had to squeeze your hand as hard as possible—and sometimes the ball would still roll out.

But Nick wasn't going to give up on his first assignment, so he took a big bottle of linseed oil that he found in the corner of the office and started working on the gloves the way his father had taught him. First, he rubbed them with the oil until the leather was supple to the touch, then he threw a ball into the webbing as hard as possible at least thirty times, and finally he shoved the ball deep into the pocket and tied up the mitt with a towel.

He had just finished the last one and was wondering what he should do next when Mr. Churchill came back into the office and glanced at the large pile of towel-wrapped gloves, one eyebrow raised.

"You've done all that since I've been gone?" he asked.

"Yes, sir," Nick said. "I'll unwrap them tomorrow. They

won't be totally broken in, but they should be better."

Mr. Churchill shook his head. "You're an industrious little guy." He picked up a clipboard and a pen from his desk. "Since you did so well with the gloves, here's something more fun. I'm putting together the roster cards, and I need the full names and birthdays of everyone on the team."

Nick stared at the clipboard, his eyes widening. "I get to talk to the players?"

"Of course," Mr. Churchill said. "I mean, you were practically our mascot before . . ."

His voice trailed off, but Nick knew what he meant. Before Nick got sick he had always come to the team's home games, and sometimes he had even warmed up with his father on the field. But maybe things were different now—he certainly wasn't going to be tossing a ball with his father anytime soon.

"Okay," Nick said. "How many players are there?"

"Twenty," Mr. Churchill said. "So if you count any more than that, you should get your eyes checked because you're seeing double."

Nick smiled and then picked up the clipboard and walked out to the field. It looked smaller without the crowd. The team was in the midst of batting practice, and most of the players were scattered around the outfield, but Satch and a few of the other veterans were sitting in the dugout. Nick took a deep breath and then marched over to them. He had met Satch once during his previous season in town two years earlier—his father had introduced him after a game—but Nick had been so overwhelmed that he was unable to utter a single word.

Satch was in the middle of a story when Nick reached the dugout, his long arms flapping as he reached the climax.

"Yeah, I pitched against that kid DiMaggio. He was play-ing for the Seals out of that Pacific Coast League, and he came up to me before the game and said that scouts from the Yankees were watching so I should take it easy on him. He got a single off me, but I struck him out twice and popped him up once. I heard that after the game those scouts sent a telegram back to New York that said, 'Joe got a hit off Satch so he's ready for the bigs.' And now they say he's going to start next season in Yankee Stadium. Just because he got a little single off old Satch."

As the story ended, Satch looked at Nick. His eyes dropped to the metal brace, and Nick suddenly wished he hadn't worn shorts. "Hey, kid," he said. "What's the matter with your leg?"

"I had polio," Nick said.

"And you can't walk without that bear trap?"

"Not without a big limp."

Satch shook his head. "Well, I saw you walking over here and you had a limp anyway. So what's the difference?"

"The doctor said I should wear it."

"I'll tell you something about doctors," Satch said, one long finger wagging. "They don't know nothing about nothing."

Nick didn't know how to respond, so he held up the clip-board. "I'm supposed to get everyone's name and birthday. For the roster cards."

One of the other players in the dugout glanced at Satch and then rolled his eyes. "Oh, this will be good."

Satch leaned forward, a twinkle in his eye. "Listen, kid. How old would you be if you didn't know how old you were?"

Nick squinted his eyes, puzzled. "Is that a riddle or something?"

"Maybe," Satch said. "Or maybe an answer."

"You don't know your birthday?"

"I have a lot of birthdays. If you asked the government, I'm born in September or August or February of 1908. Depending."

"What if I asked your mother?"

Satch shrugged. "My mother would say that baseball is an almighty sin, so I don't pay her no mind."

Nick thought for a second and then picked up his pen. "I'm going to put down August 15, 1908. If that's okay with you."

"I know you've got a job to do," Satch said. "But I can't let you lie on that form. So I think you should put down a question mark."

"Why?"

Satch leaned forward again, but this time his voice dropped. "Because mystery is good, kid. And because I want to be the only man in the world that nobody knows nothing about . . . except that I'm the greatest pitcher ever to pick up a ball."

Nick gave him a last look and then carefully wrote in the ledger: "Satchel Paige—???" Satch stood so he could see the paper and then smiled.

"Thanks, Hopalong," he said.

Nick gave him a confused look. "Hopalong?"

"Because of your brace. You kind of hop along. And I was always partial to those stories about that cowboy Hopalong Cassidy." Satch paused, a satisfied grin spreading across his face. "I've given enough nicknames in my life to know a winner. And I do believe that one's a guaranteed champ."

CHAPTER FOUR

BOTTOM *of the* SECOND

Nick finished gathering the information from the other players in the early afternoon—everybody else gave him their birthdays without any trouble—and Mr. Churchill said that he was finished for the day. His father was still working with a few of the younger pitchers, so Nick walked home alone. When he turned down the driveway, he saw Emma standing in the yard. She was wearing a baseball mitt and tossing a ball onto the slanted roof of the cabin and then catching it when it rolled off.

"Hey," Nick said. "What are you doing?"

Emma shrugged, her eyes focused on the lip of the roof as she waited for the ball to drop. "Playing catch."

"With a cabin?"

"Well, boys around here won't play catch with a girl, and the girls all like hopscotch and those other stupid games. And I used to throw with my dad, but he ran off. So now I play with the cabin."

"Oh." Nick paused. He hadn't played a real game of catch since before he got sick—a month earlier one of the orderlies at the hospital had taken him outside with a glove and a ball, but a doctor had caught them and sent them back upstairs before they could actually throw. Part of Nick was scared; he didn't want to find out that he was so bad that he'd never be able to pitch again. But the other part missed playing baseball so much that it felt like a constant, dull ache in his stomach.

"I'll play catch with you," Nick finally said. "But only if we don't talk."

She gave him a funny look. "Why can't we talk?"

"It's just a rule we have," Nick said. "Me and my dad."

"Okay," she said.

Nick went inside the cabin and got his glove out of the bottom of his duffel. Emma was standing in the middle of the yard when Nick returned, and they stood about fifteen feet apart. Nick carefully set his feet at an angle so he wouldn't have to move his bad leg to catch and throw. Although Nick expected her to throw him a lollipop—that was his father's word for a soft toss—she whipped her arm forward and gunned it right into his chest.

"Good throw," Nick said.

"I thought we weren't talking," she said.

Nick smiled and then threw the ball back. It felt weird not to move his feet, but the ball snapped off his fingers the way he remembered and cracked into her glove. After a few more tosses, Nick began to settle into the rhythm. This was why he and his dad didn't like to talk when playing catch; after a while the motion would become automatic and your mind would wander to a quiet, relaxing place. Sometimes the simple act of throwing a ball could make all the stress and clamor of the world disappear.

After fifteen or twenty minutes both of their throws started getting a little erratic, and Nick realized that they were getting tired.

"Thanks," he said to Emma as he flipped the ball to her a final time.

"You want to go get ice cream?" she asked. "My mom gave me a dime."

"My dad doesn't want me to leave the cabin," Nick said.

She wrinkled her brow. "That's what you said yesterday. But you left anyway and we had fun, right?"

"Yeah," Nick said. "But he was really mad."

"Come on. It will be fun."

Nick thought for one more second and then tossed his glove on the porch. Maybe he was going to get in trouble again, but he was still upset from the night before—and technically his father hadn't said anything about staying at the cabin before he left the ballpark.

"I think ice cream is my favorite food," Emma abruptly said, breaking Nick's train of thought.

"It's not really a food," Nick said. "It's dessert."

"Then it's my favorite dessert. What about you?"

Nick thought for a moment. "I like ice cream in the summer. Chocolate cake in the winter."

"My mom makes the best chocolate cake," Emma said. "She's a good cook. You should come over for dinner sometime."

"I'll have to ask my dad," Nick said.

They were silent for a dozen steps. Emma glanced at Nick out of the corner of her eye. "What's he like?"

"Who? My dad?"

"He used to be my favorite player on the team. I like catchers."

"He's a great catcher," Nick said. "But it's hard when you get older. My dad says it's like owning a car. . . . No matter how fast it is, eventually the shocks will wear out and the engine will start to sputter."

"You think he's going to be a starter this year? Or is Double Duty going to take his job?"

Nick shrugged. He didn't really want to talk about that—or even think about it—so he changed the subject. "I got to talk to Satch today."

Emma grabbed his arm. "You did not!"

"I did. Mr. Churchill told me to get the birthday of everyone on the team, and Satch wouldn't tell me. I think he likes being mysterious."

The words tumbled out of her mouth. "What was he like? Were his hands big? Did he say anything funny?"

"He was . . . different." Nick paused. "He gave me a nickname."

"Really? What?"

"Hopalong."

"Like the cowboy from the comics?"

"Yeah. Because of the way I walk with my brace."

Her forehead wrinkled. "That's kind of mean."

"It's just baseball," Nick said. "Guys are called Fats and Stumpy and Goofy. There's even a guy who played for the Tigers called Stinky."

"Stinky?" She was quiet for a moment. "I wish Satch would give me a nickname."

Nick just smiled. A minute later they reached Bismarck's small downtown. The ice-cream parlor was on the first block of Main Street that had stores, and they went inside and peered through the foggy glass at the assortment of flavors. After a long bout of deliberation Emma got chocolate and Nick chose strawberry. When she finished paying, they went outside and sat on the curb, frantically licking so the ice cream wouldn't melt and run down onto their hands.

"Thanks," Nick said when he was down to just the bottom half of his cone. "They had ice cream at the hospital, but it was really bad."

Emma looked at him, puzzled. "How can ice cream be bad?"

"It tasted sour. And there was something wrong with the freezer because it always had this icy fuzz on the top."

As Emma wrinkled her nose, a pair of kids emerged from the general store across the street. Nick recognized them immediately—it was Tom and Nate, two of his old friends from school.

"I've got to get home," Nick said. "If I'm not there when my dad gets back, he'll kill me."

He stood, popped the last bit of his cone in his mouth, and then hobbled as fast as he could back down Main Street. Emma caught up to him after a few steps. She was practically skipping to keep up with his pace.

"What's wrong?" she asked.

"Nothing," Nick said.

"Was it those kids?"

"Nope. I just can't be late. Not two days in a row."

Emma stopped. "I'm supposed to meet my mom down here."

"Okay," Nick said over his shoulder. "Thanks again for the ice cream."

Although Nick could feel Emma's eyes on his back as he continued walking away, he resisted the urge to turn around. She was right. Nick hadn't realized it until the moment he saw Tom and Nate, but he wasn't ready to see any of his old friends from school. They would stare at his brace and ask him questions about the hospital and whether or not he could pitch again—it would be a reminder of how much his life had changed since that fateful day when he woke up with a fever. And Nick wasn't ready to deal with that. Not yet.

When Nick was halfway home, he noticed a state police car pulled over on the side of the road behind a silver convertible. As he got closer he realized that Satch was sitting on the curb as a sour-looking policeman tore through the convertible's glove box.

"Hello, Mr. Paige," Nick said when he reached the convertible.

Satch glanced at him and then smiled. "No need to mister me, Hopalong," he said. "Ain't nobody who don't call me Satch."

The policeman looked up from the glove box. His voice was gruff: "Get out of here, kid."

Nick took a few steps down the sidewalk and then stopped. Something was wrong with the scene, but he couldn't quite figure it out: Maybe it was the look in Satch's eye or the set of the policeman's jaw. Nick didn't want to get in trouble, but he wasn't just going to walk away—not before he knew what was happening.

"What did he do?" he asked as he slowly turned around.

Nick was looking at the policeman, who gave him a glare that could have frozen a lake in the middle of the summer. Satch spoke slowly, his Southern accent making the words seem like drops of molasses.

"This fine officer of the law thinks that I stole my own car," he said.

"I don't *think* you stole the car," the policeman said. "I *know* you stole the car. Because no colored man in this state owns a fancy convertible."

"Didn't you see him at the baseball game?" Nick asked. "He was sitting in the back of this car when Mr. Churchill drove him to the pitcher's mound."

"I don't like baseball," the policeman said.

Nick just blinked, shocked into silence. Satch shrugged. "There ain't no accounting for taste," he said.

The policeman finally finished digging through the glove box and slowly straightened, his frosty eyes focusing on Nick. "You say you know this man?"

"Everyone knows him," Nick said. "He's Satchel Paige!"

"He plays for Mr. Churchill's team?"

"He's the star of the team!" Nick knew his voice was getting louder, but he couldn't help himself. "He might be the best pitcher in the world!"

The policeman gave Nick a last look and then turned and flipped the car keys back toward Satchel. They landed in a puddle.

"I'll be watching you," he said to Satch. "So don't get uppity."

A moment later he was back in his police car, and he violently pulled away from the curb, leaving behind the acrid smell of scorched rubber. Satch slowly stood up and fished his keys out of the puddle, an indescribable expression on his face, and then glanced at Nick.

"You need a lift?" he asked.

"Sure," Nick said. His house was only a few blocks away, but he certainly wasn't going to turn down a ride in a convertible—especially a convertible driven by Satchel Paige. He opened the door and hopped onto the leather seat. The silver knobs on the dashboard glittered in the late afternoon sunlight, and the engine growled as they accelerated. Nick closed his eyes as the warm summer air whipped through his hair. This was a moment he hoped he would remember.

"I had a cousin who got polio," Satch said after a minute.

Nick opened his eyes. "What happened to him?"

"He died. But that was a long time ago. Back when I was a kid."

"I know I'm lucky," Nick said. "But I still miss baseball. I always wanted to be a pitcher like you."

Satch smiled a cocky smile. "There ain't no pitcher like me." The smile slowly faded. "Why can't you pitch?"

"You can't pitch on one leg," Nick said.

Satch shook his head. "There are lots of things in life that you aren't supposed to be able to do. People told me a black kid couldn't make no money in baseball. People told me anyone born Down the Bay was going to die there. People told me I was going to go straight from reform school to jail. But I didn't pay any of those people no mind, and that's why I'm driving a silver convertible that made some cracker cop so jealous that he just had to pull me over."

Nick wanted to let Satch keep talking, but they had reached the house. "This is it," he said, pointing at the driveway.

The car coasted to a stop, and Nick got out and carefully closed the door. "Thanks for the ride," he said.

Satch revved the engine and then looked up at Nick, the jaunty half smile on his face again. "Here's a piece of wisdom for you," he said. "Ain't no man can avoid being born average, but there ain't no man got to be common."

And with those parting words he and the convertible were gone in a swirl of dust.

CHAPTER FIVE

TOP *of the* THIRD

Before his father woke up the next morning, Nick pulled out the small scrapbook he had made two years earlier. Satch's first game had been against Jamestown, Bismarck's biggest rivals in North Dakota, and he had gone straight from the train to the field. The old park had been so packed that people were practically standing on top of one another to watch. Satch somehow managed to shake off the stiffness from his long trip north and threw a complete game—with eighteen strikeouts and just one walk— and Bismarck won in the bottom of the ninth.

Six weeks later Bismarck seized the state championship in a three-game series against that same Jamestown team, and Satch pledged to return the following spring. But, of course, he never showed up. It seemed awfully funny to Nick that Satch had ended up back on the team this season—and that Mr. Churchill had given him another chance—but Nick had learned in his short life that adults changed their minds for all sorts of crazy reasons. And frankly Nick didn't care; he was just glad he was going to be able to watch Satch pitch, no matter what the reason.

Nick's father awoke when the sun hit the edge of his bed. He ate his usual pregame breakfast: fried eggs with bread, and water instead of his usual coffee because he said coffee made him too jittery to hit a good fastball. When they were finished eating, they cleaned up, and then Nick put on a pair of baggy pants because he was tired of people staring at his brace. On their way to the park Nick carried the bag again. This time it was less painful; maybe his body was getting used to the routine.

As usual they were the first to arrive, and they waited by the gate, his father nervously pacing back and forth until Mr. Churchill arrived with the keys. Nick followed Mr. Churchill to the office while his father went to the field to stretch and check his equipment.

"This town has been buzzing since Satch arrived," Mr. Churchill said when they were inside the little shack. "It's going to be a good crowd today." He looked at Nick. "Forty cents a ticket, ten cents for kids. How much money do you think we're going to make?"

"How many people do the new bleachers hold?"

"We can cram six thousand people into this little park," Mr. Churchill said. "After that either the stands will collapse or the ground will swallow us up like a whale."

Nick thought for a minute, trying to do the math in his head. Not many kids bought tickets to the games—they would either try to sneak in like he and Emma had or peek through the holes in the fence—so he multiplied five thousand adults times point four and added it to one thousand kids times point one. Which was . . .

"Two thousand one hundred dollars," Nick said.

Mr. Churchill raised an eyebrow. "That's very exact. Do you like numbers?"

"Just statistics," Nick said. "Baseball statistics."

"Of course," Mr. Churchill said with a laugh. He turned and pointed at a stack of paper in the corner.

"Those are the new programs," he said. "Your job is to sell them for ten cents. And I expect half of that pile to be gone by the end of the game."

Nick gave the pile a doubtful look—it was pretty big. "I'll try," he said.

Mr. Churchill shook his head. "Don't try. If you want to sell something, you've got to *know* you can do it. You've got to believe you're giving people an opportunity."

"An opportunity?"

Mr. Churchill's voice rose. "Those people should understand that it would be crazy not to buy this program. For a mere ten cents they can own a genuine collector's item . . . a timeless memento to prove to their grandkids that they were at the park the day the great Satchel Paige returned to town."

"It sounds pretty good when you put it that way," Nick said.

"Of course," Mr. Churchill said. "You put a pig in a nice enough dress and people will be lining up to kiss it." He patted Nick on the shoulder. "Now go out there and convince those people that they need our programs."

❋   ❋   ❋

The stands were empty when Nick got to the field, so he chose a spot near first base and settled down to watch the teams warm up. Bismarck was taking batting practice, and Nick glanced at the program to help identify a few of the players. Moose Johnson, a feared slugger with forearms thicker than Nick's thighs, was standing at his position in left field and joking with Joe Desiderato, the reliable third baseman. A couple of the local players were playing pepper just past first base. And Red Haley, a shortstop with a lightning-fast glove, was playing long toss with Satch in center field.

Red was from America but the program listed him as Cuban, which Nick had heard was a way for black players to be able to join segregated leagues. Nick didn't really understand why some people didn't want black players and white players to be on the same team—or why black players couldn't play Major League Baseball—but he also knew North Dakota was different from some other parts of the country. After all, black stars had been playing in the local leagues for years. But it was also true that aside from baseball, North Dakota was pretty much just one color—the only black family in all of Bismarck were the Spriggses. Nick had gone to school with the youngest Spriggs boy, who was so quiet that people sometimes thought he was a mute. His father worked for the railroad.

Just as batting practice ended, a stocky man in a plain gray suit walked onto the field, a bag slung over one shoulder. Satch noticed him and shouted from center field, his voice carrying clearly in the warm air: "I didn't know we were so hard up for players that we were going to sign Baby Quincy again!"

Nick took another look at the man. He had a round face and legs as solid as oil barrels, and suddenly Nick realized that he was Quincy Trouppe, the catcher who had split time with his father the previous two seasons. Nick had assumed that Quincy wasn't going to come back since the team had signed Double Duty Radcliffe, yet here he was—and no team really needed three catchers. Nick glanced at the far side of the field. His father was carefully strapping his chest protector to his body, his eyes locked on Quincy. Although his face appeared perfectly neutral, Nick knew that look—it was the same expression he had gotten one time when a man had bumped into Nick's mother on the street and said something rude.

But Nick didn't have much time to think about his father or Quincy Trouppe, because the crowd started streaming into the stadium, and from that moment he was entirely focused on selling the programs. By the time Satch threw his first pitch, Nick's voice was hoarse, but he had gotten through only half his stack. Although Nick knew he ought to wander through the stands and keep trying to sell more, he couldn't keep his eyes off the field—not with Satch pitching. He therefore slipped into one of the few empty seats in the whole ballpark. As he settled down Nick realized that this was the first baseball game he'd seen in more than a year. It certainly beat listening on the radio.

The first inning passed in a blink: Satch struck out the side on ten pitches, and the Bismarck batters made solid contact but hit it right at the opposing fielders. In the top of the second, Satch gave up a soft single to the leadoff batter. The next two pitches were both in the dirt, and Nick's father couldn't get down fast enough to block either one of them before they skipped to the backstop. Suddenly the opposing runner was standing on third base—the cheapest kind of triple—and the crowd was muttering. As Satch yelled something into his glove and then glared in for the sign, Nick's heart was beating so fast that he could hear the thump in his head.

The next pitch was a fastball. The batter swung from his heels and the bat made a dull crack. It was a lazy pop fly to center field, but deep enough for the runner to tag and score, and just like that Satch had given up his first run of the new season. As Satch stalked back to the mound, a figure emerged from the dugout—Quincy Trouppe, wearing his catcher's gear.

Quincy was halfway to home plate when Nick's father noticed him. He gave a quick, furious glance toward the dugout, and then his shoulders slumped and he walked straight off the field toward the office. The crowd was applauding, and Nick knew it wasn't a tribute to his father for the years he had played for the team. It was a sarcastic thank-you to Mr. Churchill for taking him out of the game.

Although Nick was too upset to really enjoy the remaining innings, Bismarck started to play to its potential. Satch gave up only one more hit, and the bats came alive in the fourth and fifth innings and turned the game into a rout. When the last out settled into Moose Johnson's mitt, Nick leaped to his feet and raced to the exit to try to sell a few more programs. Most people passed him without even making eye contact, and he had begun to despair when he noticed a small crowd forming around the base of the stands. Nick fought his way against the tide and found Satch standing in the middle of the group.

"Nickel for an autograph," Satch said, waving a pen.

People were digging through their pockets, searching for scraps of paper, and suddenly Nick had an idea.

"Get today's program signed for only twenty cents!" Nick shouted. "A souvenir of the time you saw the great Satchel Paige pitch live and in person!"

As Nick waved the programs over his head, Satch gave him a quick glance. And then he smiled broadly.

"It's a can't-miss opportunity," he said. "They charge a dollar for signed programs out California way, so you're getting the deal of the century."

"I'll take three," said a man to Nick's right.

"Me too," said another voice.

For the next fifteen minutes Nick struggled to make change as Satch's pen sped across the programs as authoritatively as his fastball rocketed toward the plate. When the crowd was finally gone, Satch tucked the pen back in his pocket and looked at Nick.

"What's my cut?" he asked.

"We sold fifty programs," Nick said. "Ten cents for Mr. Churchill, five cents for you, and split the other five cents down the middle." He closed his eyes as he did the math. "That's three dollars and seventy-five cents for you."

"Easy money," Satch said as Nick counted the change into his giant hand. "Let's do it again, kid."

He winked and a moment later was gone. Nick walked back toward the office, the remaining change a heavy ball in his pocket. He had only a few programs left—and had made Mr. Churchill an extra dollar twenty-five with the autographs—so he was feeling pretty good as he approached the shack. But then he heard his father's voice booming from inside.

"I played too hard for you, Churchill," he was yelling. "There weren't no need to embarrass me like that."

Mr. Churchill's voice was quiet and calm. "It was going to be more embarrassing if I left you in that game, Ben."

"I ain't done. I got a lot more ball left in me."

"Nobody's saying you don't. But I've got two younger catchers and a team that can play with any team in the country—major league included. So . . ."

There was a long pause. When Nick's father spoke again, his voice had lost its energy. "What do you want me to do?"

"I want you on my bench. You know these local teams, you can read pitchers, and if Double Duty or Quincy gets hurt, I'll need you. But that's the best I can offer."

"I'll have to think about it."

"I know you could pick up with someone else," Mr. Churchill said. "But I hope you stay. This could be a real special season."

Footsteps clumped toward the door, and Nick ducked into the shadows of the shack. He caught a glimpse of his father's face as he emerged—his skin was bright red and the muscles of his jaw stood out like two tight knots. He strode past Nick, his eyes focused straight ahead, and Nick waited until he was out of sight before emerging from the shadows. On the one hand Nick was mortified that his father had yelled at Mr. Churchill, but he also understood his anger. Nick had learned what it was like to have baseball suddenly taken away from you, and he knew the game was everything to his father—it was the only good thing in his life now that Nick's mother was dead.

Nick leaned against the shack, his mind racing. If his father really quit the team, they'd probably go back to the tiny mining town where Nick's grandparents lived. And that would be a disaster, since most people there spoke only Croatian and none of the kids liked baseball. The three days they used to spend with his grandparents at Christmas had always felt like three weeks; Nick would rather go back to the hospital, where at least they had a radio and some nice doctors and nurses, than live in a place like that.

CHAPTER SIX

BOTTOM *of the* THIRD

When Nick got home, his father was in the yard turning a huge branch into firewood with the efficiency of a sawmill. He was trimming the smaller branches from the main trunk with a hatchet—chips of wood flying in all directions—and then sawing the branches into perfect foot-long pieces that he could split into quarters with the ax. He must have been working since he got home because his shirt was drenched in sweat and the ground around his feet was colored tan by sawdust.

Nick sat on the porch and watched him for a few minutes before it occurred to him to help. He got the canvas satchel from the cabin and started gathering the perfect chunks of firewood, carrying them inside, and stacking them neatly by the iron stove. His father gave no indication that he noticed Nick, but Nick didn't mind the silence. Nothing that his father said when he was in one of his moods was likely to be nice.

Nick had been working for about half an hour and was unloading the satchel into the wood rack by the stove when he heard a yelp from his father followed by the loud thud of something slamming into the wall of the cabin. Nick dashed outside, moving as fast as he could on his bad leg. His father was bent over at the waist, clutching his left thumb with his right hand. Something dark was dripping from his fingers, and Nick felt his throat clench as he realized that it was blood. He reached up and grabbed a clean shirt from the clothesline and then hopped over to his father and held it out.

His father glanced at the shirt and then at Nick, his eyes dark and angry. "Where's your head? Don't waste a good shirt on blood."

Nick went back to the clothesline and traded the shirt for a sock with a hole in the heel. When he got back, his father snatched the sock, wrapped it tightly around his thumb, and then stared accusingly at the saw, which was lying on the ground next to the wall of the cabin.

"Want me to get a doctor?" Nick asked.

"I've spent enough money on doctors," his father said. "And I'm certainly not paying for a house call."

"Doesn't Dr. Burnhill treat the players for free?"

"I ain't on the team," his father said, his voice a low growl. "And I'm worth nothing to Mr. Churchill with a bum thumb." He looked at Nick and shook his head. "We've got to be the sorriest pair in North Dakota. Nothing but damaged goods."

"That isn't fair," Nick said quietly.

His father rolled his eyes. "Life isn't fair. Not for people like us. And you better stop dreaming and figure that out

BOTTOM OF THE THIRD

because otherwise you'll end up hungry like those farmers outside town. Or, worse yet, a washed-up ballplayer with a dead wife and crippled son."

The last words slammed into Nick's stomach like a punch, and although Nick bit his lip to keep water from spilling out of his eyes, his vision still got blurry. His father gave him a long look, a strange expression on his face, and then turned on his heel and marched out of the yard toward town. Nick hoped he was going to see the doctor after all, because one of the older brothers of a kid at school had cut his thumb on a saw and died a few weeks later of tetanus. And while his father could be mean, Nick still didn't want him to get tetanus.

It was at moments like this that Nick most missed his mother. With every passing year he remembered fewer details about her, but in his memory everything had been different before she caught tuberculosis. His father had certainly changed at her funeral as if someone had thrown a switch. He didn't laugh anymore, ever, and he talked to Nick only when he was mad or giving instructions. At least they had shared baseball before Nick got sick, but now that Nick couldn't pitch they had nothing. In fact, his father didn't even want him around—Nick was sure of that. Maybe he looked too much like his mother, or maybe he was just an unpleasant reminder, as his father said, that *life wasn't fair*.

"Are you okay?"

The voice cut across the yard. Nick looked up and saw Emma walking toward him, a towel slung over her shoulder.

Nick wiped his face on his shirt. "Yeah. I'm fine."

"What happened to your dad? My mom said he was

walking toward town with his hand wrapped in a bloody sock."

"He cut his thumb with the saw."

"All the way off?"

"Nope."

"I've got an uncle who's missing two fingers on his left hand. But he got them shot off in the war."

"You talk a lot," Nick said. He felt bad the moment the words came out of his mouth, but Emma just smiled.

"Not usually," she said. "But I like talking to you. Maybe it's because you actually listen."

Nick didn't quite know what to say, so he just looked back at her. After a moment her cheeks turned red. "I'm going swimming," she said after an awkward pause. "Want to come?"

Nick shook his head. "I haven't swum since . . . well, you know."

"What? Do you think you forgot how to do it or something?"

"No," Nick said. "It's just . . ."

As Nick's voice trailed off, he considered her offer. While he didn't really want to go swimming—or do anything other than sit on the porch—he knew if he stayed at the cabin, he was just going to feel sorry for himself.

"Fine," he finally said. "I'll go."

Whenever Nick had gone swimming, it had always been in the Missouri River, which was wide enough in most spots that not even Moose Johnson, who had the best arm in the Bismarck outfield, could throw a ball from bank to bank. Just south of town, where the dark water slowed, a giant sandbar had formed, and kids would splash around in the shallows during the warm summer months. Sometimes they would even play stickball in the sand using a worn rubber ball and bare hands.

But Emma led Nick in the opposite direction, into the dusty plain that stretched northwest of the town. They passed two abandoned farmhouses, their windows boarded up and roofs sagging, and then turned off the road and cut through a field filled with burned-out cornstalks. Emma scrambled over a small wall, pausing at the top to give Nick a hand, and when they plopped down on the other side, they were suddenly in a green field—an island of life amid the dust and dirt. Nick paused and poked a small squash with the toe of his shoe.

"Why is this stuff growing?" he asked. "I thought there was a drought."

"That's how I found the swimming hole," Emma said. "But it's supersecret, so you can't tell anyone. Promise?"

Nick shrugged. "I don't know anyone to tell. Except Satch and my dad. And I don't think they care."

Emma laughed, probably because she thought it was a joke. But it wasn't. Before Nick got sick, he had taken for granted that every day when he got out of school there would be a dozen kids waiting for him to play baseball or go swimming or walk down to the five-and-dime store to look at bikes, but now . . .

"Over here," Emma said loudly.

She had walked ahead of him and was cutting into a little stand of trees. As Nick followed her into the shade, the air became cool and moist, and he took what felt like his first deep breath in a very long time. Emma skirted the trunk of a giant tree, and suddenly a small pool of water appeared ahead of them. It was about half the size of a baseball infield, and its edges were covered with lily pads and a few thick stands of reeds.

"This is my favorite spot in the whole world," Emma said. She turned and pointed at the giant tree. "And look!"

Nick turned and saw a thick rope hanging down from one of the branches. The end was just a few feet off the ground, two thick knots standing out like mice swallowed by a snake, and he realized that it was a swing.

"Isn't it great?" Emma asked.

"Yeah." Nick glanced back at the little pond. The water appeared inky in the shade. "Who else knows about it?"

"The farmer, I guess."

"No other kids?"

"Nope." Emma pointed at the far side of the pond. "There's a path that leads to a house, but I've never seen footprints on this side of the water."

"It's amazing," Nick said. "Like an oasis or something."

Emma just smiled and then sat on a rock and pulled off her shoes. Nick went down to the shore, pushed aside a lily pad, and dipped his fingers in the water. It was cool but not cold. A few fat frogs watched him from farther down the bank, their eyes wide and unblinking.

"Last one in is a rotten egg!" Emma called.

Nick glanced up just in time to see her go swinging past him on the rope. She whizzed out high above the pond and then let go with a yelp and plummeted into the dark water. The splash almost reached the shore, and Nick stood up to get a better look. She was underwater for a few seconds, and then her head popped out, her long dark hair plastered against her white cheeks.

"Come on," she said. "Don't be a chicken."

Nick took off his shoes and then waded a few feet out into the water to retrieve the end of the rope, which was still swinging slightly from Emma's plunge. He slowly walked the rope back up next to the tree and then stood motionless, gathering his courage. Emma had clutched the rope with her hands and feet, but Nick didn't trust his bad leg to help him.

"Now or never!" Emma called.

Nick stared at the pond. "I'm worried about my brace."

"It'll dry." She paused. "Baaawwwk!"

Nick gave the pond one last look and then clutched the top knot and lifted his feet. The ground sped by, followed by water, and then suddenly he was soaring up into the air like an eagle swooping up from a field after missing a rabbit. A shout burst from Nick's lungs near the top of his arc, and he released the rope and suddenly was falling down, down, down, until he landed with a splash. He panicked for a moment when he felt the weight of the brace pulling him deeper, but after two quick strokes with his arms, he emerged from the water, laughing. Emma was watching him from shore, a satisfied smile on her face.

"It's like flying," Nick said as he waded onto the bank.

"I know," she said. "And it's all ours."

Nick tried the swing a dozen more times and only stopped because his hands were getting sore from gripping the rope. He particularly loved the moment just after he let go, when his body was hanging in midair and for a second he was flying—no bad leg, no angry father, nothing.

When they finally walked back to the house, they were the happy kind of quiet, the only noise coming from Nick's squeaking brace. His skin felt slimy from the pond.

"Thanks for taking me," Nick said when they were back in the yard. "It was kind of a bad day."

"I thought so," Emma said. "You looked sad sitting on the porch."

Nick just grunted. Emma gave him a last smile and then turned and skipped to her house. As Nick turned and slowly walked back to his cabin, it occurred to him that most kids would have asked more questions or tried to figure out why he had been upset. But Emma was different; she knew enough to leave him alone. At that moment Nick realized that he'd been wrong earlier when he said he didn't have any friends in town. Of course, it was kind of funny that his one friend was a girl—Nick had barely talked to girls before he got sick. But Emma liked baseball and had shared her secret spot with him and was really nice about his leg. And those were the kinds of things friends did.

Nick's father got home after the sun had set, his thumb neatly wrapped in a bandage. He tossed a loaf of bread and a can of beans at Nick as he came through the door and then went and lay on his bed. Nick made a fire, and when he was finished cooking, he offered his father a thick slice of toasted bread spread with the beans and a little bit of bacon fat from the jar over the stove. But his father just grunted and rolled away toward the wall.

Nick therefore had too much food, and he ate until it felt like the beans were starting to climb back up his throat.

When he was finished cleaning, he lay on his cot. He had a few blisters on his palms and a large sore patch on his leg from where the wet brace had chafed against his skin, and the pain was nagging enough to keep him awake until long after his father's snores had started to echo around the cabin. The excitement of swimming and the subsequent happy glow had helped Nick forget how the day had begun, but now he couldn't keep himself from wondering what was going to happen. Would his father really quit the team? Were they going to stay in Bismarck? He prayed they would—and not just because Satchel Paige was going to spend the summer pitching a mile down the street from their cabin. During the months Nick had spent at the hospital, it had felt as if his life had been frozen, and these first days in Bismarck had seemed like the beginnings of a thaw. And as Nick drifted off to sleep, he realized that if they could just stay here for a while, it might even begin to feel like a home.

CHAPTER SEVEN

TOP *of the* FOURTH

After breakfast the next morning Nick's father started putting on his uniform pants. Nick watched him for a long moment, trying to keep himself from asking the question, but eventually he couldn't help himself.

"Are you going to practice?" he asked.

His father glanced at him, annoyed. "I'm on the team, ain't I?" He stood and flicked his head at the duffel bag with his equipment. "Grab that."

"Yes, sir!" Nick said.

Nick couldn't keep a stupid smile off his face all the way to the ballpark. His father knocked on the door of the office and then glanced at Nick, his nostrils flaring and a thin sheen of sweat on his forehead.

"Stand up straight," he said. "How many times do I have to tell you?"

As Nick shifted the bag on his shoulder and pushed the top of his head toward the sky, the door swung open and

Mr. Churchill stepped outside. He glanced from Nick to his father.

"You coming to work or saying good-bye?" he asked.

"Coming to work," Nick's father said. "If that's still okay."

Mr. Churchill smiled and clapped his father on the shoulder. "Of course it's okay. I'll be grateful to have you on that bench."

"I always thought I might get into coaching someday," Nick's father said. "Just didn't figure it would be so soon."

"The only certainty about plans is they change," Mr. Churchill said. "Which explains why I've got to run to the dealership for a minute."

"You want me to warm up the team?" Nick's father asked.

Mr. Churchill nodded. "Yeah, have them do some running. Except for Satch—he's going to be late." Mr. Churchill turned to Nick. "And why don't you sweep the dugout? . . . That way you can watch a little bit of practice. Does that sound good?"

"Very good," Nick said.

By the time Nick got the broom out of the storage shed, Mr. Churchill had sped off in his car and the team was jogging in the outfield. Nick was halfway through sweeping the home dugout when Satch strolled onto the field. He was wearing a pair of olive pants and a white collared shirt rather than his uniform, and he looked at Nick, a funny glint in his eye.

"This is the reason a body should never be on time," he said. "I'd hate to be out there running around like some kind of jackrabbit."

"Aren't you worried about your legs?" Nick asked.

Satch shook his head. "My legs are just fine as they are. Probably because I don't generally like exercise. I believe in training by rising gently up and down from the bench."

Nick wasn't sure whether Satch was joking or not, so he focused on sweeping a little pile of sunflower seeds and dirt into his metal dustpan. After a long moment Satch threw his head back and laughed.

"Jeez, Hopalong," he said. "You're a regular chatterbox, aren't you? Just never shut up."

This time Nick knew Satch was kidding. "I *was* wondering about something," he said tentatively.

"Shoot."

"Why do people call you Satchel?"

"Why do you think?"

"I read in the newspaper that it was because your feet are so big that people said they looked liked satchels."

Satch snorted. "My feet ain't got nothing to do with my nickname. But once folks get it in their heads that a feller's got big feet, pretty soon they start looking pretty big." He gave Nick a glance. "Did you have a nickname before I started calling you Hopalong?"

"My friends used to call me Smoke. Back when I could pitch."

"Because you put heat on your fastball?"

"Yeah."

Satch's head suddenly whipped around and he stared at Nick, an eyebrow raised. "Wait, what's this nonsense about not being able to pitch? You didn't believe me when I said you could pitch on one leg?"

Nick shrugged. "I don't know any pitchers with polio."

"I know a lot more pitchers than you," Satch said. "And not all of them are as perfect as me and my normal-size feet. You ever hear of a big old farm boy called Three Finger Brown?"

"Of course," Nick said. Mordecai Brown had been a famous pitcher who played for a bunch of teams before the First World War. He had gotten his nickname because he had only three fingers on his pitching hand, which supposedly helped him throw the best curveball of his day.

"Then let me ask you this," Satch said. "You think Three Finger would have gotten famous if he decided to quit ball after sticking his hand in that wood chipper? You think we'd know his name if he just decided to stay on that farm and feel sorry for himself?"

"I guess not," Nick said, his voice low. "But my dad says you can't pitch on one leg, and he knows a whole lot about baseball."

"Your daddy may know plenty," Satch said. "But there ain't no man alive who knows more about pitching than old Satch, and I'm telling you that you can pitch on one leg or no legs or with three fingers or twelve. All that matters is that you know how to miss the fat part of the bat."

Nick glanced at the outfield. The team had stopped running, and his father was tossing a ball with a few of the younger pitchers. He was probably telling them to step into their throws and make sure their wrists snapped as the ball left their fingers—the same advice he'd given Nick a million times.

"Over here, kid," Satch said, snapping his fingers. Nick looked back at him. "I can tell you don't believe me, but I've got a way to change your mind. You're coming on a drive with me. Right now."

Nick gave the bench a long look—he desperately wanted

to go with Satch, but he had barely started sweeping. "Mr. Churchill wanted me to finish this before he got back. And my dad will be mad if I leave the park."

"I'll let you in on a secret," Satch said. "Your daddy works for Mr. Churchill, and Mr. Churchill will pretty much do anything to keep old Satch happy. And right now what would make Satch happy is if you come with him. Okay?"

"Okay," Nick said.

The silver convertible sped down a dirt road outside of town, moving twice as fast as Nick's father ever drove a car. Nick clutched his seat, a combination of scared and exhilarated, as the wind whipped his hair and his blurry eyes tried to focus on the bouncing landscape. Satch glanced at him and then laughed, the sound muffled by the whipping wind.

"You look just like my wife," he said. "She's fit to pass out every time we go for a drive."

"Is she here in Bismarck?" Nick asked.

Satch rolled his eyes. "Please . . . that woman lasted one day in this little town before turning around and hightailing it back to Pittsburgh. Not enough black folks around these parts for her—and not enough shopping, neither."

"There are a bunch of stores downtown," Nick said.

Satch laughed again, this time slapping his leg and leaning back in his seat. Nick wished he would keep his eyes on the road. "Most women's idea of a shopping district isn't a gas station and a five-and-dime," he said when he finally caught his breath. "You'd better learn that before you get too much older."

"I don't know anything about women," Nick said.

"Then here's a piece of advice. There are lots of things a woman will say she loves before she marries you. She might pretend she likes to run around the country and go to jazz clubs and watch your games, but the moment that ring lands on her finger—oh boy, you sure find out the truth right quick."

"How did you realize that you wanted to marry her?" Nick asked.

Satch stared out the windshield, a funny half smile on his face. "Well, there aren't a lot of women who would put up with old Satch. Maybe for a night or two, but eventually they all get tired of . . ." His voice trailed off. "I guess what I'm saying is that Janet's an awfully patient woman. Even if she couldn't stand to be in Bismarck for more than twenty-four hours."

The convertible slowed. As they rattled over a cattle guard, Nick glanced out the window. They were passing a worn Office of Indian Affairs sign, and his stomach contracted as he suddenly realized where they were.

"This is the reservation," he said.

Satch arched an eyebrow. "You got something against Indians?"

"No. I've just never been out here."

"Then be ready," Satch said. "These people are poor as dirt. Reminds me of Down the Bay."

"What's Down the Bay?"

"The neighborhood where I grew up. Part of Mobile." Satch's lips were tight, the words not rolling out of his mouth the way they usually did. "These folks on the reservation would starve if the government didn't send them food. But it's no fun to eat old cheese and beans seven days a week."

They came over the top of a small hill and a small settlement appeared: a cluster of tents surrounding a little wood house. The dirt road ended near the closest tent, and as Satch turned off the engine, three men watched them from the shadows of the house. They were wearing a strange mix of clothes—beads and worn buffalo hide and other traditional Sioux gear that Nick recognized from his books at school, but also wool army jackets and leather boots. They must have been hot beneath all those layers.

"Why are they wearing army clothes?" Nick asked as Satch opened his door.

"Because that's what the government sends them."

As Satch stepped out of the car, Nick took a deep breath. He wanted to stay in his seat, but he knew it would be rude so he forced himself to get out and walk over to Satch's side. The three Sioux men were walking toward them, and Nick felt as if he could feel other eyes spying on him from the shadows of the tents. White people never came out to the reservation—there had been a kid in school who claimed his father had taken him once, but nobody had believed him.

"Are you sure this is okay?" Nick asked. "I heard they don't like visitors."

"I'm not a visitor," Satch said. "I'm practically family. In fact, they made me an honorary chieftain. Their medicine men tell a story about how I brushed back an evil Indian commissioner with a Rising Tom and saved the tribe."

"Really?" Nick asked doubtfully.

"If I'm lying, I'm dying," Satch said with a broad smile.

The three Sioux men reached their side. "Hello, Long Rifle," the oldest one said. His hair was gray, but his eyes were as black as ink. "Are you here to hunt?"

"Not today," Satch said. "Just deer oil. And maybe a drop of something to light a little fire in my belly."

One of the other Sioux men pulled out a clear bottle filled with a brownish liquid. He handed it to Satch, who uncorked it and drank. As soon as Satch swallowed, he bent over, his fists clenching and the veins in his neck standing out like ropes.

"Whooo, boy!" he said when he straightened. His voice was raspy. "That's as fine as any of the moonshine down south."

"Take what you want," the older man said.

Satch shook his head as he handed back the bottle. "I generally believe that too much of a good thing ain't hardly enough, but I'm supposed to be pitching tomorrow. Not to mention that I always believe in setting a good example for youngsters." He glanced at Nick. "Remember that, kid. One sip is medicine. More than that is slow poison."

"Yes, sir," Nick said.

Satch looked back at the Sioux men. "I'll be needing two bottles of deer oil today. One for me and one for my friend here."

"I got a new batch in my tent," the older man said. "Follow me."

Satch and the three Sioux headed through the camp, Nick trailing a few feet behind them. Although Satch looked like he was walking slowly, his legs were so long that both the Sioux and Nick had to hurry to keep pace. They stopped in front of a large tent on the far side of the camp, and the oldest Sioux man went inside. Nick stood close to Satch, his eyes scanning the surrounding landscape. Down the hill from the camp was a small lake. The coals of what must have been a huge bonfire smoldered on its shore, and a tent made of animal hides stood a dozen feet from the water. A man wearing only a simple loincloth had pulled a large stone out of the coals and was dragging it toward the tent with a pair of giant iron tongs.

"What's that?" Nick asked, pointing.

Satch turned and looked. "Medicine hut," he said. "They put that hot rock inside and then one of their magic men throws hot water on it until the tent fills with steam. You sit in there for ten minutes and you'll be hotter than a sheepdog in the bayou."

"Why do they do it?"

"They say you can see things in those huts. Visions of your life." Satch paused. "The government men want these people to give up their religion, so they hate those huts. Trust me, if a government man comes around here, that tent will disappear faster than Cool Papa can run from first to third."

Nick's brain tripped on the last bit of Satch's sentence. "You know Cool Papa Bell?"

Satch smiled broadly. "Know him? I've played with the man. In fact, there ain't no ballplayer worth a busted nickel who hasn't played with old Satch."

"Is he really as fast as they say?"

"Is Cool Papa fast? That boy could turn out the lights and get in bed before the room got dark. I've seen him hit a ground ball up the middle that hit him in the chest as he was sliding into second base."

Nick could feel his forehead wrinkling. "Is that true?"

"Depends," Satch said. "There's book true and there's baseball true."

"What's the difference?"

"There are thousands of people who would swear on the Bible that they saw that ground ball hit Cool Papa. And maybe it happened that way or maybe it didn't, but the important thing is that it *feels* true. Because Cool Papa is the fastest man ever to play the game."

"Faster than Ty Cobb?"

"Faster than Cobb?" Satch snorted. "Don't take this personally, but a black man is always going to be faster than a white man. That's just a hard fact of life. A white man running against a black man just ain't going to cut it. That's like asking a bulldog to keep up with a greyhound."

Just then the Sioux man emerged from the tent clutching two glass jars filled with a yellowish liquid. Satch pulled a small wad of bills from his pocket and separated out a few dollars. As the two men traded the money for the jars, Nick stared at the liquid. It might have been his imagination, but it seemed like it had an evil tint.

"What is it?" Nick asked when he couldn't contain his curiosity any longer.

"Magic potion," Satch said. "Folks come out to the ballpark because they want to see Satch pitch, so I've got to be ready every day of the week and twice on Sunday."

"And that stuff helps?"

"It keeps my arm as fresh as a baby." Satch handed one of the jars to Nick. It was slick on the outside with grease, and Nick had to clutch it tightly to keep it from dropping. "Use it on your bum leg. Just rub it in and wait for the heat."

"My doctor said that medicine won't help," Nick said.

Satch rolled his eyes. "Doctors and religious folk will both tell you the same thing. . . . Their way is the only way. But the truth is that there's more than one road in life. You understand what I mean?"

"Yeah." Nick gave the liquid another glance. "I'll give it a try."

Satch patted him on the shoulder. "Good. But be careful with that stuff. First time I used it, my arm nearly jumped out of the room."

A few hours later Nick was staring at the jar again, only this time he was back in the cabin. He had taken off his brace and was sitting on his bed wearing just his underwear, and as he stared down at his legs he realized that they looked as if they belonged to two different kids—the bad one was so skinny that his knee stuck out like a doorknob. When Nick finally found his courage, he carefully unscrewed the jar. The smell hit him first, a combination of kerosene and some fruit that Nick couldn't identify, and it stung the back of his throat. Before he could second-guess himself, Nick stuck a rag in the jar, swirled it around, and then wiped his bad leg from midthigh to ankle. The smell became so intense that tears were running down Nick's cheeks, and when he finished covering every bit of exposed skin, he lay back and closed his eyes.

The sensation was gentle at first—a faint warm tingling that felt like someone gently stroking a feather against the hair of his leg. But as the seconds passed, the heat got more and more intense, until after a few minutes it felt like a battalion of fire ants was assaulting his skin in steady, vicious waves. Nick clutched the blanket under him, his fingers so tight that every muscle in his arm ached.

"Dad!" he shouted, even though he knew his father wasn't home.

Silence. The fire ants had now doused themselves in gasoline and lit a match. Nick opened his eyes and glanced down at his bad leg. It was bright red. He started to count backward from ten, promising himself that he would feel better by the time he reached zero. *Ten . . . nine . . . eight . . . seven . . .*

"Aaaahhhh!" Nick was in so much pain that he wasn't sure he was the one yelling as he leaped out of bed and dashed toward the door of the cabin. He burst outside and half fell down the stairs before grabbing the handle of the water pump with both hands. He furiously moved it up and down, his leg stuck forward toward the spigot, and as the first gush of cool water hit his skin, Nick groaned aloud in sweet relief. As he kept pumping, his skin separated into little puddles of hot and cold. It was an indescribably strange sensation. And then, just as the fire abated enough that Nick could focus on anything other than his leg, he heard a loud laugh behind him.

"What the heck are you doing?" a female voice asked.

Nick slowly turned around. Emma was standing in the middle of the yard, her arms folded across her chest and a broad smile on her face.

"I'd tell you what I was doing," Nick said, "but it would sound pretty stupid."

Emma giggled. "It can't be any more stupid than what I'm imagining."

Nick looked down and suddenly flushed as he realized that he was wearing just his underwear and a T-shirt. His bad leg was also so red and splotchy that it looked like it was covered in wet paint.

"Satch gave me some medicine," Nick said sheepishly. "It was supposed to make my leg better, but it just burned like hot coals."

"Are you sure it didn't work?" Nick gave Emma a wary glance, not sure if she was kidding. "I mean, you got all the way out here without your brace, didn't you?"

A long moment passed and then Nick's mouth fell open. *She was right.* He had run all the way from the cabin to the pump, and now he was standing in the middle of the yard without his brace as if it was normal.

"You're right," he said. "I guess I did."

Emma smiled one more time. "Well, maybe you should try that stuff again. Except next time you should probably wear some pants."

CHAPTER EIGHT

BOTTOM *of the* FOURTH

Nick's father got back to the cabin in the early evening, and as he strode inside, he glanced at Nick.

"Put on your Sunday best," he said gruffly. "Mr. Churchill needs us downtown."

Nick pulled the battered trunk out from under his cot and rummaged around until he found his old pair of dark pants, collared shirt, and leather shoes. He and his father had bought them for his mother's funeral, and at the time they had been a few sizes too big so Nick could grow into them. But that had been a long time ago, and the pants and shirt now clung to his body as if they were trying to strangle him, and the shoes pinched his toes like pliers. When Nick stood up and attempted to button his pants—a hopeless effort—his father looked at him and shook his head.

"Those are what your grandma used to call high-water pants," he said.

"Why?" Nick asked.

"Because you could wade across a stream without having to roll them up." He glanced at Nick's bad leg and then at the bed, where the brace was lying next to the pillow. "Why aren't you wearing your machinery?"

"I walked without it," Nick said. "Today in the yard."

"Don't be a fool. You keep that thing on until a doctor tells you to take it off. Understand?"

Nick nodded. "Yes, sir."

His father gave his pants another look. "Well, I guess we'd better go downtown and find you something."

The something they found turned out to be a heavy wool suit that was on sale at Woolworth's and a white dress shirt with so much starch that it felt as if it were made out of paper. The instant Nick stepped out of the store into the warm summer night, sweat began pouring from his armpits and down the small of his back, and his entire body felt like one giant itch. His father had also decided that his shoes still fit—the definition of wishful thinking—so he was hobbling even more than normal as they walked up to Mr. Churchill. He was standing on a corner at the center of town, his eyes locked on a makeshift mound that a few men were constructing in the street, and he grinned when he noticed Nick.

"You look like a priest," he said. "Do you worship at the altar of our Almighty Father or the Church of Baseball?"

"Baseball," Nick said. "Except on Sunday morning."

"Good answer," Mr. Churchill said. He reached into a satchel lying on the pavement next to him and pulled out a stack of flyers. "Easy assignment tonight. You just have to give away all of these."

Nick glanced around the street, which was quiet for a Tuesday night. "To who?"

"I'm willing to make a bet that this street is packed in ten minutes," Mr. Churchill said. "How about a nickel?"

"I don't have a nickel to bet," Nick said.

Mr. Churchill pursed his lips. "Well, it's Tuesday night so we have to make some kind of bet." His eyes focused on the flyers in Nick's hands. "How about this. . . . You give away all of those flyers and you can come on our next road trip. Otherwise, you're stuck here in Bismarck while we barnstorm across the great Midwest."

Out of the corner of his eye Nick noticed his father's eyebrows shoot up, but he didn't say anything. "Deal," Nick said.

He and Mr. Churchill shook hands, and then Nick glanced down at the top flyer. It was just three sentences printed with bright red ink: THE LEGEND RETURNS! BISMARCK CHURCHILLS PRESENT LEROY SATCHEL PAIGE, GUARANTEED TO STRIKE OUT THE FIRST NINE MEN OR YOUR MONEY BACK! TICKETS GOING FAST!

"They look pretty good, don't they," Mr. Churchill said. "And if you give them all away, we'll have a full house tomorrow."

Nick gave the street another glance. "I'll do my best."

"I already told you not to worry about finding people," Mr. Churchill said. "Believe me, I've got a whole mess of tricks up my sleeve."

The tricks began ten minutes later while Nick was standing outside the five-and-dime store trying to convince an old woman to take a flyer even though she claimed she'd never been to a game because "that little ball moves too fast." The first sign that something unusual was about to happen was the honking of a car horn in the distance. Nick turned his head in time to see two men on horseback galloping down the street. They were carrying a banner between them that read BISMARCK CHURCHILLS—TEAM OF CHAMPIONS. As they pulled up in front of Mr. Churchill, their huge horses snorting and lathered with sweat, the two men stood out of their saddles and saluted. Nick's eyes widened as he realized that it was Moose Johnson and Joe Desiderato from the team.

"Those about to play ball salute you!" they shouted in unison.

Mr. Churchill stepped forward. In the few minutes since Nick had last seen him, he had wrapped himself in a white sheet and put a wreath of leaves on his head. He looked like a Halloween version of a Roman emperor.

"Have you brought me tribute?" he asked.

"Yes," Joe replied. He spoke in a loud monotone. "We have found the greatest pitcher in all the land."

"And where can I find this gallant champion?" Mr. Churchill asked, his voice booming.

Joe turned and pointed. "Behold!"

As the word echoed off the buildings, three cars turned the corner at the end of Main Street. The first, a giant black sedan, was filled with the horn section of a band—tubas and trumpets sticking out the windows as they played a rollicking song. The second car, also a sedan, had a bunch of Bismarck players in their full uniforms hanging off the sideboards and waving at the growing crowd. The third was Satch's silver convertible. He was sitting in the back between two men dressed in outrageous silver suits, and as the convertible slowed to a stop in front of Mr. Churchill, the two men simultaneously turned their heads to either side. Huge billows of flame burst from their mouths, and Nick stared, stunned. The only time he'd ever seen fire breathers was at the carnival that set up on the outskirts of town late every August.

Mr. Churchill stepped forward, his eyes locked on Satch. "Your coming has been foretold," he said. "Are you the greatest pitcher in all the land?"

"I be the man," Satch said.

Mr. Churchill smiled broadly. "Excellent. We hear that you possess wondrous powers. Can you demonstrate a few of them for us? Your magical hesitation pitch, perhaps?"

"It depends," Satch said. "I only demonstrate my powers to true believers."

People had been emerging from storefronts and pouring out of the little alleyways that fed onto Main Street, and Satch cocked his head toward the growing crowd. The response was a loud shout and a smattering of applause. Satch smiled to himself and then got out of the convertible and walked over to the mound that Mr. Churchill had built in the street. As Satch made a big production out of stretching his arm, Nick's father emerged from the crowd, a catcher's mitt on his hand. Nick stared at him, wondering how he'd managed to get his wounded thumb into the stiff leather.

"Here it comes, folks," Mr. Churchill shouted. "The infamous hesitation pitch."

Satch started his windup, his hands going down as his leg went up, but then—right at the top of his motion—he froze, balancing neatly on one foot.

"What's the matter?" Mr. Churchill asked after a moment. "Are you scared to throw the ball?"

"Not scared," Satch said. "Just pondering."

"Pondering what?"

Satch turned his head just slightly so he could look at Mr. Churchill. "I am hesitating right now so I can cogitate on how I am going to throw my hesitation pitch."

The crowd laughed. When it was silent again, Mr. Churchill waved impatiently at Satch. "Well, don't cogitate all day," he said. "Throw a strike!"

Satch whipped his body toward the glove and the ball flashed out of his hand—maybe not his best fastball, but still moving like it wanted to get somewhere. As the ball cracked into the mitt, the crowd, which had been steadily growing, went wild. Satch bowed and Mr. Churchill gave him a proud smile.

"That was wonderful," he said. "Do you have anything else in your bag of tricks that you might be able to show this amazing crowd?"

Satch scrunched up his forehead. "Well, I have my internationally famous chicken ball."

"Chicken ball?"

"Yes, sir. The very same ball that I threw for the king and queen of England and the king and queen of Spain. And I'll tell you . . . them royalty just ate it up."

"I'd like to see a chicken ball," Mr. Churchill said. "But I don't know about the rest of these good people." His eyes scanned the crowd. "What about you? Do you want to see a chicken ball?"

This time the cheer echoed up and down Main Street— loud enough that they probably heard it all the way out on the Indian reservation. Satch smiled and then ambled back to the mound. When he was in position, he bent over at the waist, staring in at Nick's father. He made a show out of shaking off the first sign—and the second—but he nodded firmly at the third and then came to a set, his glove at his chest and his eyes glaring at the catcher's mitt. His leg moved back and his hands rose as if he were starting his windup, but then he paused and returned to the set. The crowd muttered. Satch took a breath and then his leg and hands moved again, but again he stopped.

Nick glanced around him at the crowd—people were leaning forward, mouths open, totally focused on the lanky man standing on the makeshift mound. Nick looked back just in time to see Satch start a third windup. He paused again, and the crowd grumbled, louder this time, but then Satch's leg kicked up and his arm whipped toward the catcher's mitt. Nick looked for the ball, his eyes straining in the twilight, but instead he saw a strange, floppy figure flying down the street—

It was a *rubber chicken*. It made it halfway to Nick's father and then skidded to a stop in the dirt, its legs akimbo and neck twisted at a strange angle. One of the horn players from the band made a strange sound with his instrument—a *bawk, bawk, bawk*—and suddenly the crowd erupted with laughter. People were slapping their knees and bending over and pointing at the chicken, tears running down their faces. It was absolute pandemonium.

"Ladies and gentlemen, you saw it right here in downtown Bismarck," Mr. Churchill bellowed. "The infamous chicken pitch! And if you want to see more amazing feats, come on down to the ballpark tomorrow, where you can see these fine boys play the best ball anywhere in the Dakotas. Heck, maybe the best in the world."

The brass band started playing and the crowd pressed

toward Satch, and for the next twenty minutes Nick was giving away flyers as fast as his hands could move. He finally ran out just as the crowd was reduced to dregs. Mr. Churchill was still talking to a few people, but Satch was getting into his convertible, alone. Nick walked over to him.

"That was pretty funny," he said when he was within earshot.

Satch looked at him and grinned. "I figured it would go over like gangbusters. This is a farm town, and farmers are the same everywhere. Simple folk like simple jokes."

"You've done this before?" Nick asked.

"Only in every little town south of the Mason-Dixon Line. And it didn't matter if the crowd was black or white. . . . If they were the kind of folks who knew the business end of a chicken, they'd laugh." Satch gave Nick a look. "Churchill said you were trying to give away a mess of flyers."

"Yup," Nick said. "And I gave away all of them, which means I get to go on the next road trip."

"Good." Satch paused. "And what about that deer oil? You try it?"

"It felt like someone set fire to my leg," Nick said. "But I walked without my brace."

Satch smiled again. "Attaboy. We'll get you back on that pitching mound yet."

Nick nodded, but he didn't really believe it—there was a big difference between running out of a house because your leg was burning and playing baseball. But it was awfully nice that someone thought he could be a pitcher again. Especially since that someone knew more about pitching than anybody for hundreds and hundreds of miles.

CHAPTER NINE

TOP *of the* FIFTH

Nick awoke the next morning with a smile on his face. Every day that he got to see Satch pitch felt like Christmas, but today was particularly special, since the flyer had promised that Satch was going to strike out the first nine men or the fans would get their money back. His father left for the ballpark right after breakfast, but Nick still had to do the chores, so he rushed through sweeping the cabin and cleaning the ash from the stove. When he was done, he sat on his bed with his pants rolled up staring at his brace. Fragments of his doctor's orders echoed through his head: "The correction will happen gradually. . . . It's important to stick with the program. . . . Don't push yourself too far or too fast. . . ."

Nick undid the straps of the brace, tore it off his leg, and shoved it deep under his cot. He rolled down his pants to disguise his decision and then limped out of the cabin before he could second-guess himself. For the first half of the walk to the ballpark he was too excited and nervous to really notice how his leg felt, but as the adrenaline gradually wore off, he began to pay attention. It was kind of like the sensation you got when you'd been carrying a heavy bag for a while and then put it down—good, but also weird. As he got close to the ballpark, Nick stumbled a few times as his knee got tired, but he didn't mind. The feeling of freedom was worth it.

Mr. Churchill was standing by the door of the office when Nick arrived, a big smile on his face as he looked at a line of people that had already formed in front of the ticket booth.

"Standing room only today," he said as he gleefully rubbed his hands together. "I can feel it." He glanced at Nick. "You think you can match what you did with the programs last time?"

"I'll try," Nick said.

Nick got the programs from the office and then returned to his previous position near home plate. By the time the team finished batting practice, the stands were already full and he'd sold most of his thick stack. Nick had occasionally glanced at the bull pen next to the home bench, where Satch was warming up, and he'd noticed that Satch seemed more serious than usual today—he wasn't joking with the other players or focusing on anything other than Quincy Trouppe's mitt.

As Satch walked out to the mound at the top of the first inning, a buzz ran through the ballpark. Nick squatted next to the railing, as close to the field as he could get, the programs once again forgotten by his side as the leadoff batter settled into a crouch. The first strike was a blur of a fastball on the outside corner. The second strike was a curveball that broke so sharply that the batter ducked out of the way before the ball nicked the inside corner of the plate. And the third strike was another outside fastball, which the overmatched batter swung through before turning around and trudging back toward the dugout.

And that was how the first three innings went. Satch wasn't showboating or joking or messing around—he was throwing pure gas so accurately that Quincy never had to move his mitt more than an inch or two. Nick watched the show, totally mesmerized. There was an art and a rhythm to the way Satch pitched: The ball moved up and down, inside and outside, and just when a batter seemed to think he'd figured out the pattern and guessed a pitch, Satch would adapt. The first eight men struck out on just thirty pitches—with only two foul balls—and as the ninth man walked toward the plate like a condemned prisoner, the crowd rose to its feet.

"Come on, Satch!" Nick heard himself yelling. "One more!"

Satch started off with another fastball on the outside corner. The batter swung, almost apologetically, but somehow the bat managed to find leather and with a sickly *crack* the ball sliced toward right field. Nick and everyone else gasped as they tracked its flight, trying to figure out if it would be fair or foul. And then it landed, right next to the line, and the umpire's voice rang around the park: "Foul ball!"

The batter couldn't have touched the next two pitches if he'd been swinging a barn door, and as the third strike slapped into Quincy's glove, the crowd roared. Satch was already walking off the field, and he tipped his cap as he took his seat on the bench.

"Unbelievable," a man sitting next to Nick yelled. "I wouldn't believe it if I hadn't seen it with my own two eyes!"

The next innings felt like a carnival, and Nick sold his last program in the bottom of the eighth with Bismarck leading 12–0. He was terrified of losing the money he had collected before the end of the game, so he went back to the little office, where he found Mr. Churchill sitting at his desk, a cigar sticking out of the side of his mouth.

"Aren't you supposed to be managing?" Nick asked.

Mr. Churchill smiled. "I'd say they seem to be managing just fine without me." He cocked his head to the side. "Listen to that. You hear it?"

Nick listened for a long moment. "The crowd?"

"That's the sound of satisfied customers. We offered them a deal today that they couldn't lose. . . . Either they got to see baseball for free or they got to see something great. And Satch sure gave them something great. Now these people are going to go home and tell all their friends about what happened here today, and we'll be sold out for the rest of the season. That's an absolute guarantee. Because nobody wants to miss the chance to see something special."

Nick just nodded. After a short pause he reached into his pocket, pulled out all of the dimes and nickels he had gotten from selling the programs, and put them in a big pile on the desk. His pants felt ten pounds lighter when he was done. Mr. Churchill looked at the pile and smiled.

"You keep this up and you're going to have to come to my lot and start selling cars," he said. He picked out one of the nickels and slid it across the desk. "Go buy yourself a pop. My treat."

"Thank you," Nick said as he returned the nickel to his pocket.

Mr. Churchill flicked his head at the door. "You better go fast or you'll miss the end of the game."

Nick bought a Coke from the booth beneath the bleachers and then went up into the stands. A good portion of the crowd had left after Satch had come out of the game in the seventh inning, leaving lots of empty seats, and he chose a spot near third base. The Coke was so cold that it had little flecks of ice stuck to the glass bottle, and Nick relished the fizz on his tongue and the quick rush of sweetness. The last time he'd had a soda was at Christmas, when the hospital gave them out as a special treat.

Barney Morris pitched the top of the ninth. He had a good fastball—although obviously not as good as Satch's—and he would mix in a knuckleball to keep the hitters confused. Nick loved the unpredictability of the knuckleball and had tried to throw it back when he was pitching, but his hands hadn't been big enough yet for the grip. He glanced down at his fingers, wondering if that was still true, and missed the final pitch—another swinging strikeout, the seventeenth of the game for the opposing team's overmatched batters.

As the crowd flooded toward the exits, Nick allowed himself to be carried by the tide. He dropped the empty Coke bottle into a crate near the gate and then stood motionless for a moment, wondering if he should go back to Mr. Churchill's office for another assignment. Just then someone bumped into him from behind, and Nick stumbled forward. He tried to catch himself, but his bad leg buckled and he rolled into the dirt.

"Sorry," a voice said.

Nick pushed himself to his feet before looking to see who had knocked into him. And then he froze—it was Tom and Nate, his old friends from school. They were staring at him, their mouths hanging open.

"Hey," Nick said. His voice sounded high in his ear.

"Hey," Tom said as Nate continued to stare. "We thought you were still at the hospital."

"I got out yesterday," Nick said. He didn't mean to lie, but he also didn't want to admit that he had been in Bismarck for almost a week.

"Are you . . . better?" Tom asked.

Nick hesitated. "Yeah."

"My mom said you almost died," Nate said, the words coming in a rush. "She said the doctor told her that you had the highest fever he'd ever seen."

"I don't know," Nick said. "I don't remember much about being sick."

In the awkward pause that followed, Nick decided that he had been right about not wanting to see his old friends—it was just too weird. Life in Bismarck had kept moving along, and now he was just a stranger whose name they happened to know. Nick was about to say good-bye when a familiar face emerged from the gate of the stadium: Emma. She smiled when she noticed him and walked over to their little group.

"That was amazing," she said. "I don't think Babe Ruth could have hit Satch today."

Tom and Nate turned their wide-eyed stares to her as if she were some strange alien that had swooped down from the sky—they probably weren't used to hearing a girl talk about baseball.

"Yeah," Nick said after an awkward moment. "He was great."

Emma's hand touched his arm. "My mom wants to know if you and your dad want to come over for dinner sometime."

"Maybe," Nick said. "I'll have to ask him."

"Okay." There was another awkward pause. "Well, I'll see you back home."

Emma turned and headed back down the lane toward the house. Tom and Nate watched her walk until she was out of earshot, and then both of their heads whipped toward Nick.

"Why were you talking to her?" Nate asked.

"She's my new neighbor," Nick said.

Tom raised an eyebrow. "You never used to talk to girls."

"She's nice. And she likes baseball."

"Is she your girlfriend or something?"

"No!" Nick said. "She's just my neighbor."

Nate elbowed Tom, a grin on his face. "Maybe that's really why he went to the hospital. He caught cooties from a girl."

"Well, that part's true," Nick said. "It was the worst case of the cooties they'd ever seen. They had to give me shots and everything."

Tom and Nate both laughed, and Nick felt a sudden rush of relief. Maybe everything wasn't so different after all.

"So when are you going to start pitching again?" Tom asked.

Nick felt the smile disappear from his face. "I don't know. I figured I'd have to wait until next season."

"No way," Nate said. "Remember when Alex broke his leg? He got to join a team in the middle of the summer."

"I forgot about that."

"We need a good pitcher," Tom said. "So . . ."

"Sure," Nick said. "I'll think about it." But that was another lie—no matter what Satch had told him, Nick knew he couldn't pitch, not if his bad leg couldn't even hold him up when a kid bumped into him from behind.

CHAPTER TEN

BOTTOM *of the* FIFTH

Nick wasn't sure whether Mr. Churchill had meant what he said about letting him travel with the team, but two days later when his father returned from practice, he pulled the duffel out from under his bed and tossed it on the cot.

"Pack," he said. "We leave tonight."

Nick tried to keep from glowing as he grabbed some clothes. He had always imagined that barnstorming would be a grand adventure—traveling from town to town to play local teams in front of crowds who rarely saw strangers. He had just finished packing when the sound of a car horn echoed from the street, and his father grabbed the duffel and walked outside. Nick followed, making sure to close the cabin door tightly. A blue Plymouth Sedan and green Chrysler Airflow were parked in front of the house. Mr. Churchill and the white players were stuffed into the Plymouth—it was so full that it looked like a door might pop off—and Satch and the five other black players were in the Chrysler. Bags were lashed to the roofs of both cars with thick cords.

"Hop on in," Mr. Churchill shouted. "The road calls!"

Red Haley opened the back door of the Chrysler, and Nick and his father squeezed inside. Satch turned around and grinned from the front seat.

"Next stop Fargo," he said.

From the moment Nick got in that car seat, his life felt like a blur. The team played nine games in seven days in eight towns. They headed east to Fargo and then south from Watertown to Sioux Falls to Sioux City to Norfolk to Fremont to Grand Island to Hastings. The towns and games quickly blended together, and Nick wouldn't have remembered any details except that Mr. Churchill told him to record every statistic that he could find.

And so Nick knew that by the time they rolled into McPherson, a town near the center of Kansas, they had traveled 987 miles while compiling an unbeaten record of 9–0. Satch accounted for six of those wins, giving up only four runs—three on a fluke double that Moose Johnson lost in the sun—and striking out forty-five batters. The team's bats were also hot, and they collectively hit .322 with six home runs and fifty-two runs scored. In fact, they were so impressive that by the end of the game in Sioux City, the home crowd had been cheering for every Satch strikeout or diving play made by Red Haley.

But Nick kept some unofficial statistics too, and by those measures the crowds were getting a little bit nastier with every mile they drove south. People were yelling names from the stands at Satch and the other black players—names Nick had never heard—but he knew they must be bad because once when he turned around on the bench to look at the person who was shouting, his father had put a firm hand on his shoulder.

"Don't give that idiot the satisfaction," he said.

They pulled into McPherson late on a Friday night—the game in Hastings had taken more than three hours because Bismarck put men on base in every inning. Nick was sitting in the back of the Chrysler with most of the black players, and as they pulled up in front of a ramshackle hotel in the center of town, he noticed that a group of men across the street were staring at them.

"Those people don't look very friendly," Nick said.

Red Haley glanced over at them and shrugged. "Life on the road, kid," he said. "You should see how they treat us in Cuba. Satch near got killed one night out in the country."

Satch glanced up from untying the rope that held down the trunk's flap. "That's no joke. Those people were lighting up a bonfire to roast old Satch about the time I slipped out of town."

"What did you do?" Nick asked.

"It was a language problem," Red said.

Satch laughed. "Yeah. See, they speak Spanish down there, and I don't know more than ten words. But I always like to play along when people talk to me. So one night we lost, and after the game a guy came up and was talking in Spanish, fast as a typewriter. I figured he was telling me how well I pitched, so I just kept nodding my head."

"Except he was a mob boss," Red said. "Who had lost a lot of money betting that we would win."

"He sure was sore about losing the money," Satch said. "But he got even more sore because it turned out he was asking me whether I had thrown the game."

Red burst out laughing. "And there was Satch, nodding and smiling like he'd just pulled the perfect con."

Satch laughed too. It was a funny story, but Nick was too preoccupied with the men across the street to smile. They were clustered together, talking quietly and occasionally glancing at Satch and Red. Something about their expression made the hair on the back of Nick's neck stand up, and as soon as Satch finished untying the trunk's flap, Nick grabbed a bag and hurried into the hotel. But it turned out that things were just as uncomfortable inside—Mr. Churchill was standing at the front desk, his face bright red.

"You ought to be embarrassed," he was half shouting at the skinny desk clerk. "My boys are playing tomorrow in this town, and they deserve a place to sleep."

"I'm sorry," the clerk said in a tone that made it clear he wasn't sorry. "It's just a rule."

Mr. Churchill's hand slammed against the desk. "It's a ridiculous rule. And I won't stand for it!"

"I don't know where you're from," the desk clerk said, his eyes narrow. "But around here we do things our way. And we don't take to white folks and colored folks sleeping under the same roof. Understand?"

"Then I'll take my business elsewhere," Mr. Churchill said.

The clerk shrugged. "You'll get the same answer from every hotel in town."

Mr. Churchill turned away from the desk, his hands on his

hips and his mouth pursed. Satch and Red had come into the hotel just in time to hear the last few lines.

"We're driving back to Hastings," Mr. Churchill said. "I'm sure some hotel up there will be happy to take our money."

Satch shook his head. "There's no sense in driving all the way back there. Not with a game here tomorrow."

"We'll skip the game."

"No game, no money," Satch said. "And we sure didn't come to McPherson just for the lovely company."

Mr. Churchill still looked uncertain, and Red stepped forward. "This ain't our first rodeo," he said. "We'll find a place to sleep. Sometimes there are boardinghouses or other colored folks who will take us in for the night. It usually comes with a good meal, too."

Satch glanced at the small restaurant adjacent to the lobby of the hotel. "Definitely better than the pig slop you get in a dump like this."

He said it loudly, and the desk clerk's head whipped around. Red noticed and grabbed Satch by the elbow. "Let's go," he said. "Before those boys outside decide to stick their nose in it."

"It's just not right," Mr. Churchill said, shaking his head. "We're a team."

"Right don't have nothing to do with it in a town like this," Satch said. "Now, you go upstairs and go to sleep and don't think on this for one more minute."

Red and Satch started toward the door. Nick's father, who had been standing silently near the desk during the entire exchange, looked at Nick.

"Come on," he said.

Satch paused and looked at Nick's father. "You and your boy ain't colored. Unless there's something in your family history that you haven't told us."

Nick's father avoided Satch's gaze. "I'm not staying if my teammates can't stay."

"I appreciate it," Satch said. "I surely do. But we might end up sleeping outdoors, and your son . . ."

Nick's father and Satch both looked at Nick, and he tried not to squirm under the attention. "He'll be fine," Nick's father finally said. "He's a tough kid."

Nick's mouth fell open—that was the first nice thing his father had said about him in a long time—and he was still glowing a minute later when they all piled back into the Chrysler.

"You know anywhere around here?" Satch asked Barney Morris as they pulled out into the street. "We got about two minutes before it's dark."

"Nope," Barney said. "Looks like we're staying in the Cornfield Ritz."

Satch smiled. "Greatest hotel room God ever created."

They drove until the lights of the town had faded behind them and then pulled off into a field. Nick's father got a bunch of towels from the equipment bag, which they rolled up to use as pillows, and Nick lay down on a little patch of grass between the rows of corn and yanked his jacket over his torso like a blanket. It had been a long day of carrying bags and running for water and shagging balls, and he felt himself drifting off to sleep as soon as his eyes closed. The last thing he remembered was the sound of a harmonica and the laughter of Satch and a few of the other men.

Nick awoke before sunrise, shivering because the coat had fallen off him in the middle of the night. He wanted to get a little deer oil from the car and rub it on his leg before everyone woke up—that had been his routine during the trip—but Satch was standing a dozen yards away, lit by the bluish glow of the dawn as he stretched his neck. He looked so tired that his face was almost drooping at the edges, and when he noticed that Nick was awake, he stared at him for a long moment, the usual twinkle gone from his eye.

"They ain't hitting nothing today," he finally said. "*Nothing.*"

CHAPTER ELEVEN

TOP *of the* SIXTH

The game against McPherson started at one. It was a perfect afternoon for baseball—blue skies and just a hint of a breeze blowing out toward center field. The field had only a basic grandstand, but it was packed by the first pitch, and as Nick put the tar and a rag out by the warmup circle, he realized that the men who had been standing across the street the previous night were sitting directly behind home plate. When he mentioned that to Satch, who was carefully lacing his shoes on the bench, Satch just smiled.

"Good," he said. "They'll have the perfect view to watch me embarrass their team."

In the top of the first, Red made it to second base with two outs. Moose got a fastball on the inside corner that he muscled into left field for a sharp single, and Nick's father, who was coaching third base, waved Red home. The throw was late and the catcher also appeared to bobble the ball,

but the umpire called Red out. As Satchel and the rest o.
defense trotted onto the field, Mr. Churchill waddled ou
home plate. Nick, who was rearranging the bats, was cl
enough to hear the exchange.

"Just call it fair," Mr. Churchill said. "That's all I ask."

The umpire waved a finger in Mr. Churchill's face. "You
come up and talk to me again and I'll have the cops drag you
off this field. We don't put up with bellyaching in this town."

Mr. Churchill stared at him for a long moment and then
just nodded to himself and returned to the bench. After Satch
finished his warm-up, McPherson's first batter, a skinny kid
with pale skin, carefully dug into the box. Satch's first pitch
was a curveball that snapped sharply just before it reached
the plate. The batter swung wildly, missing the ball by at
least a foot, but before Quincy could throw it back to Satch
the McPherson player turned and looked at the umpire.

"That ball is funny," he said.

As the crowd hooted, the umpire tapped Quincy on the
shoulder. "Let me look at that."

Quincy shrugged and handed him the ball. The umpire
made a big show of inspecting it before turning and throwing it toward the home team's bench. He pulled another ball
out of his pocket, and after he handed it to Quincy he stared
out at the mound and wagged his finger again.

"Keep it clean," he said. "None of your big-city tricks
down here."

Nick expected Satch to get mad, but instead he just smiled
a smile so wide that his teeth glinted in the midday sun.

"You may as well throw 'em all out because they're all
going to jump like that!" he shouted.

The umpire ignored him and settled back behind Quincy, his eyes dark behind his mask. Satch's next pitch, a fastball, cleaved the heart of the plate. Nick waited for the umpire's hand to go up, but instead his voice rang around the stands. "Ball one!"

Satch turned on the mound and stared at Mr. Churchill, his hands on his hips. Mr. Churchill responded by hopping up as quickly as Nick had ever seen him move and striding across the diamond toward the opposing bench. The umpire took a few steps forward to intercept him.

"What did I just tell you?" the umpire asked, his face red. "Stay off my field!"

Mr. Churchill ignored him and pointed at the opposing manager. "You find a real ump or me and my boys are getting in our cars and leaving."

"One more word and I'm calling in the cops," the umpire said. He waved at the stands near third base, where three giant deputies were standing, their arms folded across their chests.

"I'm not talking to you, greaseball," Mr. Churchill said. His eyes were locked on the opposing manager. "A fair ump. *Now.* Or we hit the road."

The opposing manager pushed himself off the bench and ambled out toward Mr. Churchill. Despite his deliberately casual walk, there was an unmistakable glint of menace in his eyes. "I think you want to finish this game," he said when he reached Mr. Churchill. He nodded slightly at the stands. "If you and your boys walk off this field, I won't be liable for what these people do."

Mr. Churchill snorted. "And then what? Do you think that

any traveling team will ever come back to this pathetic cow patty of a town if you run us out on a rail? In fact, I'll bet most folks won't even drive down your main street if they hear you were dumb enough to hire a crooked ump just so you could say you beat Satchel Paige."

"I ain't crooked," the umpire said defensively.

"Then you're blind," Mr. Churchill said. "And either way my boys aren't playing with you behind the plate. So get off this field, you dirty chiseler."

Mr. Churchill's voice had risen, and his last words carried clearly into the stands, sparking a cavalcade of catcalls. The group of men behind home plate were half leaning onto the field, their faces ugly and contorted, and the Bismarck players in the infield instinctively moved toward Satch on the mound. Nick's father got up from the bench and sidled over to the on-deck circle.

"If this gets ugly, you go stand by those deputies," he said to Nick, his voice low. "You hear me?"

Nick glanced at the three deputies, who were still standing in a cluster, stone-faced. "I don't think they're on our side."

"Of course they aren't," his father said. "But if they got a decent bone in their body, they ain't going to stand for a kid getting hurt. So you go over by them, understand?"

As Nick nodded, his father crouched down, his fingers curling around the handle of a bat. And that was when Nick got really scared; his father wasn't the kind of man who was prone to exaggeration. Nick started to sidle toward the deputies, but just as he got near home plate—

"Fine," the opposing team manager said, the word ringing

around the infield. He pointed into the stands. "Get down here, Bobby."

A short man wearing a dark suit emerged from the crowd. The deputies opened a gate in the fence, and he marched over to Mr. Churchill and stuck out his hand.

"Bob Bonner," he said. "I used to ump over in Kansas City for the regional tournaments."

"Just call it fair," Mr. Churchill said. "That's all I ask."

Bob nodded and then turned to the previous umpire and raised an eyebrow. After a long moment he tore off his chest protector and dropped it and his mask on the ground before stalking into the stands. Bob picked up the mask and then looked out at the pitcher's mound, where Satch was calmly watching the scene.

"Let's play ball," Bob said.

It turned out that Bob was as fair as the previous umpire had been crooked, and through eight innings Satch gave up only two hits—a soft roller down the third baseline and a dying quail to center field. By the top of the ninth, Bismarck was winning 5–0. With two outs and Moose at the plate, Satch strode up to the on-deck circle and lazily swung a bat a few times before taking a knee and then gesturing to Nick for a towel. When Nick reached his side, he waved a hand at Moose.

"You know how to read a batter?" he asked.

Nick stifled his surprise—Satch rarely talked to anyone during a game when he was pitching. "No, sir."

"Watch his front knee. That tells you everything." Nick looked at Satch skeptically, and Satch made a little cross over his heart. "I promise . . . that knee is like peeking at a man's cards. Is he tense because he's getting ready for a fastball? Is he sitting on that back leg because he's waiting for the curve? You read that knee the right way, and you've beaten the batter before the ball even leaves your hand."

Just as Satch finished speaking, Moose hit a hard grounder right at the second baseman, and the top half of the inning was over. As the Bismarck players started running onto the field for the last half of the ninth, Satch stepped in their way.

"Everyone stay on the bench," he said. "Except Quincy."

The team froze. Moose glanced at the stands and then back at Satch. "Come on," he said. "Not today."

"I'm going to embarrass this town," Satch said. "And boy do they deserve it."

"I want to get out of here alive," Red said.

"Me too," Moose said.

"Trust me," Satch said. "After these last three outs everyone in these stands is going to slink home without another peep." He pointed at Quincy. "Just us. Nobody else."

Everyone looked at Mr. Churchill, who just shrugged. "Better to be famous and dead than boring and alive," he said.

And so Satch and Quincy trotted onto the field, alone. The crowd had been subdued for several innings, lulled to a stupor by Satch's relentlessly overwhelming pitching, but when they realized that the rest of the team wasn't coming out of the dugout, they rose to their feet, the catcalls suddenly surging with renewed intensity. As the first McPherson batter walked to the plate, Nick shook his head; it looked strange to see a field without a single fielder other than the pitcher.

Nick glanced at his father, who was watching Satch with a hint of a smile on his face—which was surprising since he hated showboating. But maybe his father agreed with Nick that this town deserved whatever it got.

Satch started off with a fastball, and the batter swung and missed—wildly. Someone from the opposing bench shouted that he just needed to get his bat on the ball to get a hit, and he nodded to himself and shortened his grip. The second pitch was also a fastball, this one up around the bottom of his armpits, and he managed to nick the ball as it whistled past. As the batter settled into his crouch to face the third pitch, Nick followed Satch's advice and stared at his knee. He looked tense, like he was waiting to be bitten by a snake, and *curveball* flashed through Nick's mind just as Satch reared and threw. He was right—it was a curveball—and the batter was so far in front of it that he probably could have swung twice. Three pitches; one out.

The second batter tried to bunt the first pitch, but it was a breaking ball in on his hands and he skidded it foul. On the second pitch he tried to bunt again, but Satch threw a curve in the dirt and he couldn't pull his bat back in time. The third pitch he had to swing, and he was six inches under a Rising Tom. Six pitches; two outs.

The third batter was the skinny kid who had opened the game by complaining that Satch was doctoring the ball. He had a little bat—not much bigger than the bat Nick had used back before he went to the hospital—and he took a half swing at the first pitch. The ball made a dull *thwack* as it made contact with the wood, but the swing had been late and he hit a lazy little pop-up in foul territory halfway between home plate and first base. Satch trotted under it, but at the last moment he pulled his glove away and let the ball fall to the grass.

"You ain't getting off that easy," he said to the kid, loudly enough that everyone in the stands could hear him.

And he didn't. Satch's second pitch started at the kid's front shoulder, but as the kid flinched, it broke violently and caught the inside corner for a strike. The third pitch was a textbook Satchel fastball—just above the knee on the outside edge of the plate. The kid just stared blankly at it as Bob pointed his fingers to the side.

"Strike three," he said. "Game over."

As the Bismarck team flooded onto the field to congratulate Satch, Nick glanced at the angry group of men behind the plate. He expected to see them shouting things at Satch—or at least glaring angrily at the field—but instead they were filing out, heads lowered. Nick's father followed his stare and then raised an eyebrow.

"Good," he said. "Maybe next time they'll think twice before flapping their mouths."

CHAPTER TWELVE

BOTTOM *of the* SIXTH

The drive back to Bismarck took two days. They headed almost due north to play a quick game in Columbus, Nebraska—where vast oceans of cornfields stretched to the horizon in all directions—and then continued to Aberdeen, South Dakota, where Satch struck out ten men in five innings before turning the game over to other pitchers. They finally rolled back into Bismarck late at night on a Monday. Nick stumbled out of the Chrysler, wobbly with sleep, and as the two cars rolled away, Mr. Churchill waved a hand out the window.

"Day off tomorrow," he said. "Stay out of trouble."

Nick followed his father down the path to the cabin and barely remembered falling into bed. His dreams were vivid, culminating in one that he'd had many times at the hospital: He was standing on a pitching mound, everyone from school clustered around the field, and as he started his windup he would glance down and suddenly realize that he wasn't wearing any clothes other than a ratty pair of underwear. Usually the dream would make Nick nervous, but this time he awoke with a smile on his face. It was nice to be on a mound again—even if it was only a dream.

When Nick rolled over he saw that his father was eating a can of beans by the stove, already dressed. "This place needs cleaning," his father said when he realized that Nick was awake. "I'm going fishing, so meet me at the hole this afternoon once you've finished your chores."

A minute later he clumped out of the cabin. Nick stared at the broom for a long moment and then rolled onto his stomach and closed his eyes. It had been a long time since he'd slept much past sunrise, and he enjoyed the feeling of dozing in and out of consciousness until most of the morning was gone. When he finally got out of bed, he hurried to sweep the floor and clean the stove and make his bed. It was warm outside, but before Nick left he put on long pants to conceal the fact that he wasn't wearing his brace—which was still hidden deep under his cot.

Their old fishing hole was just below the railway bridge north of the center of town, where a small sandbar often formed in the eddy around the concrete pilings. The best fishing on this part of the river was for walleyes, which were lazy and liked to relax in the slack water. The summer before Nick went to the hospital, he and his father had gone almost every day there wasn't a game, and in addition to walleyes they'd caught just about every fish you could find in this stretch of the Missouri: brown trout, rainbow trout, lake trout, cutthroat trout, northern pike, chinook salmon, and a variety of catfish.

When Nick got to the hole, his father was standing thigh-deep in the water just off the closest sandbar, two buckets near him on the shore. Nick glanced in the buckets. The first one was filled with minnows for bait, but the second contained three large walleyes, their olive scales and silver eyes glittering in the sun. Nick guessed they were all about a foot long and probably weighed two and a half pounds apiece—a good catch.

"Bring me another minnow," his father said from the water. "I just lost mine."

Nick cupped a minnow in his hands and waded into the water. He staggered a bit in the current on his bad leg, but he forced himself forward until his father grabbed the minnow from his palms, hooked it in one neat motion, and cast into an eddy.

"I saw you've got three already," Nick said. "Pretty good day."

"It would be better if I could stay through twilight," his father said. "But we're having dinner with Mrs. Landry and her daughter. She invited us this morning."

"Oh," Nick said. He suddenly realized that he'd forgotten to mention Emma's invitation—or maybe he hadn't forgotten. Maybe he didn't want Emma to hear the things that sometimes came out of his father's mouth.

"Can I hold the rod for a while?" Nick asked after a long moment.

His father shook his head. "You're old enough to cut your own rod. Now go clean those fish for dinner. I'll be home in a while."

Nick was disappointed, but he just nodded and waded back to shore. It was awkward to carry the bucket home—it kept banging against the side of his leg—and by the time he got back to the cabin, he was sore and frustrated. He took his father's big Buck knife from the sheath beside the stove and cleaned and gutted the fish outside on the porch. When he was done, he washed the fillets in the pump, put them in a pot filled with cool water, and left the pot in the shade. He went to give the remains to the pigs in the pen down the street, and by the time he got back, his father was roughly scrubbing his face with a towel by the pump.

"Come get clean," he said when he noticed Nick. "We don't want Mrs. Landry thinking that we live like a bunch of savages."

Nick got a bar of soap from inside and then followed his father's example and scrubbed his face, neck, and hands. When he was done, he ran a comb through his hair—temporarily bringing order to the bird's nest that lived atop his head—and put on his cleanest shirt and pants. His father was finished about the same time, and he grabbed the pot before they walked across the yard and knocked on the back door of the house. A moment later Mrs. Landry answered. She was wearing a plain blue dress with a high starched collar. Nick, who had seen her only from a distance, had thought that her hair was tinged with gray, but on closer inspection he realized that it was actually just blond streaks.

"Come in," she said. "Everything's almost ready."

Emma was standing by the narrow staircase as they entered. She was also wearing a dress—bright red—with white socks and matching red shoes. As Mrs. Landry and Nick's father walked into the kitchen, she looked at Nick and rolled her eyes.

"I feel like a doll," she said. "I should be in a glass case or something."

"I think you look nice," Nick said.

"And you look . . . clean. What did you do to your hair?"

Nick ruefully patted the top of his head. "I tried to use a comb. Does it look stupid?"

"Not stupid," she said. "Just different." She flicked her head at the kitchen. "Come on. My mother's been cooking all afternoon."

Dinner was the best meal Nick had eaten in several years. Emma's mother fried the fish in cornmeal and served it with boiled greens and potatoes and strawberry pie for dessert. She even had a tall pitcher of cool milk—which Nick drank practically by himself—and when the meal was over, his stomach felt bloated and happy. Nick's father must have felt the same way because when he finished his pie, he turned to Mrs. Landry and smiled a smile that had existed only in the deepest corners of Nick's memory.

"That was a fine meal," he said. "Me and my boy are much obliged."

"It was no trouble," Mrs. Landry said, her hands folded neatly on her lap. "I think of you often. . . . It must be difficult to live without the kindness of female company."

"It is," his father said. "But there's no sense in complaining about it. These are tough times for lots of folks, and we do the best we can." He slid back from the table and glanced at Nick. "Now let's leave them to their cleaning."

His father was snoring twenty minutes later, but Nick had slept too late that morning to be ready for bed, so he went outside and sat on the porch. About ten minutes after the lights went off in the main house, a shadow appeared in the yard and crept toward him. It was Emma.

"What are you doing out here?" Nick asked when she was close enough that he could see her clearly in the moonlight.

She put her finger over her lips. "Quiet. Follow me."

She reached out and took his hand, and Nick let himself be led across the yard to the little bench on the edge of the trees. Her palm was warm and soft. When they were seated, she let go and then stared down at her bare feet, which were sticking out of her long nightgown.

"That's the first time my mama's had a man in the house who wasn't kin," she said. "You know, since my daddy left."

Nick didn't know what to say, so he just grunted. After a long moment she turned and looked at him, her face a puzzle of shadows. "Your mom got sick, right?"

"Yeah. Tuberculosis."

"My daddy was no account. He ran off when I was five and ended up getting killed running liquor in Michigan."

"Really?"

She shrugged. "I don't know. That's what my cousin told me. Mama says he died in a railway accident, but that doesn't sound as exciting."

In the long pause that followed, Nick let himself think—really think—about his mother for the first time in a while. She had always been the one who got him up in the morning, who made sure he ate enough for dinner, who told him to change his shirt when it was dirty . . . basically, the person who really looked out for him. His father's role had always been just to teach Nick about fishing or baseball or how to sharpen a knife, and now he barely even did that. The truth was that Nick had been on his own for the three years since his mom had died—and now that he was old enough to think about it, he realized that being on your own was exhausting.

Nick suddenly realized that Emma was staring at him, her head cocked. "What are you thinking about?" she asked.

"Nothing."

"It wasn't nothing. I can always tell when you get lost in your brain because your lips get all tight and you stare at thin air."

"Oh." Nick paused and then the words came in a rush. "Was your mom nicer before your dad went away?"

"I don't remember," Emma said. "But I think she used to laugh a lot more."

"She laughed tonight."

"She was happy tonight. I'm not used to seeing her happy."

They were quiet for a long moment. Emma was looking at her feet again. "Are we friends?" she finally asked.

"Of course."

"What about when we go back to school? Are you still going to talk to me?"

"Why wouldn't I talk to you?" Nick asked, confused.

"You didn't seem very happy that time I walked up to you and your friends at the ballpark."

Nick shrugged. "It's just . . . hard. Tom and Nate wouldn't understand about a girl liking baseball and stuff."

"Is that why you like me? Because I like baseball?"

There was a note in her voice that Nick couldn't quite identify—hurt, maybe—and some instinct told him that his answer was really important. "I don't know," he said after a long pause. "I guess I like you because you're you."

"Okay," she said. And then she stood and skipped away across the wet grass of the lawn, the words trailing behind her in the darkness. "Sleep well, Nick."

CHAPTER THIRTEEN

TOP *of the* SEVENTH

Late the next morning Nick idly swept the home bench while watching Satch take batting practice. He was a surprisingly good hitter given his lanky frame, and when he made solid contact, the ball would leap off his bat. He tended to hit line drives, which meant that he ended up with lots of singles and doubles rather than home runs, but when he really caught a pitch, he would send it a long way. He had just rapped a sharp grounder up the middle, hard enough that the pitcher had to hop to the side, when Mr. Churchill walked onto the field. He whistled at Nick, and Nick hustled over as quickly as he could.

"We got a meeting," he said when Nick reached his side. "You and me."

Nick stared at him, puzzled. "A meeting?"

"Downtown. With Wild Bill Langer."

Nick's jaw dropped. William "Wild Bill" Langer was a notorious figure. He had been elected governor four years

earlier, but he had been convicted by a federal court for some complex scheme involving taking money from highway department employees. As a result the state supreme court had ordered him removed from office, and Wild Bill had responded by barricading himself with ten friends in the governor's mansion and declaring that North Dakota was now an independent country. The drama had ultimately ended when Wild Bill decided to step down as governor and fight the case in the courts, and while Nick was in the hospital his conviction had been overturned. Now he was running for governor again and claiming that the entire thing had been a scam to get him out of office.

"Why do you want me to go to the meeting?" Nick finally asked.

Mr. Churchill smiled thinly. "Because he's less likely to eat me for lunch if there's a kid in the room."

Nick didn't find that very comforting—especially since he'd never seen Mr. Churchill intimidated by anything—but he got in the car because he couldn't think of any good excuses. They drove downtown and parked in front of the Patterson Hotel. Nick had never been inside, but he knew the building well—it was ten stories high and had been the tallest structure in North Dakota until they'd completed the new statehouse, two years earlier. As they walked into the ornate lobby, Nick stayed as close to Mr. Churchill's side as possible. Mr. Churchill nodded at several men in severe blue uniforms and then stopped in front of the giant oak reception desk.

"I'm here to see Bill," he said to the clerk.

The clerk glanced up from writing in a giant book. "Name?"

"Churchill."

"Of course," the clerk said, snapping the book closed. "Sorry, Mr. Churchill. I'll tell him you're here."

As the clerk scurried away, Mr. Churchill glanced down at Nick. "Have you ever been in here before?" he asked.

"No, sir."

"Well, what do you think?"

"It's nice," Nick said.

Mr. Churchill smiled. "It ought to be nice. They worked on this monstrosity for twenty years. Do you know why?"

"Because it was hard to build?"

"Because according to state law any property under construction is exempt from taxes. So as long as they kept working on it, they didn't owe the tax man a red cent."

"I heard they built a secret tunnel connecting the basement with the train station," Nick said. "So they could smuggle stuff inside during Prohibition."

Mr. Churchill gave him a sharp look. "And where did you hear that?"

"At school. One of the kids said his father helped build it."

Mr. Churchill was silent for a long moment and then shrugged. "Well, I wouldn't put it past them. Most of the folks who come into this building have a rather loose interpretation of the law."

The clerk suddenly reappeared at Mr. Churchill's side. "Follow me," he said. "Mr. Langer is ready to see you."

The clerk led them to a dark wood door in the back of the lobby. He knocked five times in an unusual pattern and then a lock clicked. As the door swung open, a thick burst of smoke escaped, and when Nick followed Mr. Churchill into the room, it took his eyes a moment to adjust to both the

dark and the burning haze of tobacco. He recognized Wild Bill immediately from the newspaper photographs. His hair was slicked straight back from his forehead, and he had a round face with a pronounced dimple in his chin. He stared at Mr. Churchill through intense eyes for a few seconds and then glanced at Nick.

"Hey, kid," he said. "Are you supposed to be his bodyguard or something?" There was no smile on his face or anything else to indicate he was joking.

"No, sir," Nick said. "I'm just here to make sure you don't eat him."

A smile flickered across Wild Bill's face—quick as a bolt of lightning—and the men sitting around the table with him laughed.

"I generally don't eat people until suppertime," Wild Bill said when the laughter subsided. "But I'm sure Churchill appreciates your concern." His gaze turned to Mr. Churchill. "I've been hearing a lot about your team."

"Best players money can buy," Mr. Churchill said. "At least outside of the majors."

Mr. Churchill reached for a chair, but Wild Bill shook his head. "Don't sit," he said. "I've just got a quick proposition for you."

Mr. Churchill gave the chair a glance and then shrugged. "You know me, Bill. I'm always ready to hear a deal."

"I was talking with one of my compatriots the other day," Wild Bill said, his voice rising, "and we realized that Bismarck has never won a championship in any sport. Which, we agreed, is an outrage. This city is the capital of the great state of North Dakota, and as such it should achieve glory commensurate with its stature. Do you not agree?"

"Of course," Mr. Churchill said. "But what did you have in mind?"

Wild Bill glanced at one of the men sitting with him, who pulled out a leaflet and tossed it on the table. "An old friend of mine has decided to put together a competition in Wichita, Kansas. A national semiprofessional baseball tournament. It will be played at the new stadium on the Arkansas River, and teams will travel from all over the country to compete for glory."

"And you want us to go?" Mr. Churchill asked as he picked up the pamphlet.

"I want you to win," Wild Bill said. "I want you to remind America that Bismarck and North Dakota are still on the map." His voice dropped. "And I also want you to make history. No team with both white boys and colored boys has ever taken home a trophy in a tournament like this. You and Bismarck will be in the history books. Forever."

Mr. Churchill gave Wild Bill a long look. "And what do you get out of it?"

"Just civic pride," Wild Bill said with an odd smile that Nick recognized—it was the code that adults sometimes used to signal when they weren't telling the truth. "Although it sure would be nice if your champions decided to march in one of my parades before the election."

"Oh," Mr. Churchill said. He paused. "I'll think about it."

Nick stared at the pamphlet as Mr. Churchill drove him home. It was just a grainy photograph of a man sliding into second base and a few lines of type:

National Baseball Congress Tournament

Semipro champion of the world to be crowned at the brand-new Lawrence Stadium. $1,000 cash prize to winning team!

Nick's jaw dropped when he saw the prize. You could buy almost two Studebaker trucks for that kind of money—it seemed like an awful lot just for playing baseball.

"So what do you think?" Mr. Churchill eventually asked. "Do you think we should go?"

"That's a big prize," Nick said. "I mean, if the team wins."

"It's a lot of money even if we don't win," Mr. Churchill said. "The guy who's putting it together contacted me and offered us an appearance fee."

Nick looked at Mr. Churchill, surprised. "You already knew about the tournament?"

Mr. Churchill laughed. "Knew about it? That guy has been calling me every day since the moment I landed Satch. He knows that if we show up, his stadium will be full for every game."

"Then why did you act surprised with Wild Bill?"

"Because now if we go, Wild Bill will think that he owes me a favor. And he'll also think that I take his advice, which is even more valuable."

A minute later they pulled up in front of the house, and as Nick got out of the car and walked toward the backyard, he realized that the adult world was really complicated. How were you supposed to know what was real when people were always telling half-truths or pretending they didn't know things or sometimes just plain lying? Nick wondered if he would ever figure it out—did you just turn eighteen and suddenly all of this stuff made sense? Or would he spend the rest of his life confused because he believed that there should be some relationship between what a person said and what they meant?

Nick was still lost in that thought as he walked up the stairs to his cabin, but as his hand touched the doorknob he heard a bright burst of laughter behind him. His head whipped around—Emma was standing next to a giant pile of dirt in the middle of the yard, a shovel in one hand.

"You walked right past me," she said. "Like your head was lost in the clouds."

"Oh." Nick stared at the pile of dirt. "What are you doing?"

"I built you a pitcher's mound."

"What?"

"Look. . . ." Her foot nudged a block of wood. "You can use this as a rubber."

Nick stared at the torn-up grass. "Your mother's going to kill you."

"Probably." She paused. "You want to give it a try?"

Nick took a long moment before he answered. He knew what Emma was doing—and it was really, really nice of her. But he was also scared. Ever since he first got sick, Nick had clung to the fantasy that someday he would be able to pitch again, and he knew it would be harder to believe in that dream if he got on a mound and couldn't even toss the ball to home plate without falling on his face. Yet Nick also knew he couldn't put off this moment forever. At some point he needed to try.

"Yeah," Nick finally said. "Let me get my glove."

By the time Nick returned to the yard, Emma had finished

sinking the rubber into the mound, and Nick patted down the dirt with his foot. When he finally got into his set and fingered the ball in his mitt, his hands were sweaty. Emma was crouched at the far end of the yard, maybe a few steps too close, but Nick wasn't going to complain. His mind was racing as he started his motion, but as his hands rose his instincts took over and his head cleared. The only thing in the world that mattered was Emma's glove. His body drove forward, his hips coming through the way his father had taught him, and the ball spun out of his hand. For a moment everything felt the way he remembered, but then his bad leg couldn't quite hold his weight and he stumbled a little. He managed to catch himself, and as he straightened back up he glanced at Emma. She was holding up the ball, a huge grin on her face.

"That was a strike," she said.

She tossed the ball back, and Nick tried it again. And again. And again. With each toss his confidence grew a little bit. Yeah, his left leg wasn't perfect and he couldn't drive to the plate quite as confidently as he wanted, but he was *pitching*. His father had been wrong, the doctors were wrong . . . even Nick himself was wrong. It was possible. *He could do it.*

Around the fifteenth or twentieth pitch, just as Nick's confidence reached its peak, he got the feeling that someone was watching him. He glanced over his shoulder and saw his father standing on the steps of the cabin. Nick tried to contain his excitement, but the words slipped out before he could stop them.

"Look, Dad," he said. "I'm pitching!"

His father just stared at him, and Nick suddenly felt his

confidence slipping away like air leaking from a punctured balloon.

"Yeah," his father said after what felt like an hour.

"Do I look . . . okay?"

"You're wasting your time," his father said. "Power comes from the legs. No legs, no power."

He turned and went into the cabin. Nick waited until the door was closed and then he dropped his glove and walked toward the street. He heard Emma call his name behind him, but Nick couldn't turn to look at her. Not right now.

CHAPTER FOURTEEN

BOTTOM *of the* SEVENTH

Bismarck lost the next day to a traveling team from Grand Forks. Satch pitched pretty well, giving up only two runs, but the bats were quiet and Barney Morris allowed a three-run triple in the ninth to make the final score 6–1. The players were grumpy after the game, probably because they weren't used to losing, and most of them left the park almost as quickly as the fans. Nick was cleaning up garbage in the stands when he was surprised to see Satch walk back onto the field, still wearing his uniform. When he noticed Nick, he waved.

"Get down here," he said, his voice echoing around the empty park. "I need someone to catch for me."

Nick walked down to the edge of the field before responding: "I don't have my glove."

"In the dugout," Satch said, flicking his head. "Take your pick."

There were two gloves on the bench. One was an outfielder's

mitt, so large and floppy that it covered Nick's hand like a sleeping cat. The other was smaller and stiff in the pocket—it probably belonged to someone who played second base or shortstop. Nick chose that one and then slowly walked out to home plate.

"I'm not a catcher," he said as he crouched, his bad leg stuck out to the side.

"I'm not going to throw you the Rising Tom," Satch said. "Just plain old fastballs. All you gotta do is hold that glove out and tell me if you have to move it. Okay?"

"Okay," Nick said.

Satch started his easy windup and Nick tried to hold the glove perfectly still. From this angle Satch's leg kick looked impossibly high—Nick's eye focused briefly on the sole of his shoe—and then the ball smacked into the webbing of the glove, hard enough that Nick's entire body shifted with the impact.

"How was that?" Satch called from the mound.

"Good," Nick said. "I don't think I moved it at all."

"Five more," Satch said.

The next four were exactly like the first, but the fifth was outside and Nick tried to stab the white blur with the glove. He was a little too aggressive and the ball smacked into his palm rather than the webbing. The sting came a moment later—a sharp, hot pain that felt like when his teacher at school whacked him with a ruler—and Nick instinctively dropped the glove. As he rubbed his hand, Satch wandered in from the mound.

"Sorry," Satch said. "That's exactly what was happening during the game. I kept missing my spot."

"Is something wrong with your mechanics?" Nick asked. That was something his father used to say when he was teaching him how to pitch: "Imagine that you're a car and your arm is the engine. If the mechanics of the motion are sound, everything else will fall into place."

Satch shrugged. "Nah, it's just pitching. Some days it goes okay and some days you start thinking too much and it all falls apart." He picked up the glove and tossed it to Nick. "You want to throw for a minute?"

Nick glanced at the pitching rubber. "From the mound?"

"You're a pitcher, aren't you?"

"Not anymore. My dad saw me pitching yesterday and said that I didn't have any power in my legs."

Satch was silent for a long moment, a dark shadow passing across his face. "What about the deer oil?" he finally asked. "Is that helping?"

"I put on a little every morning," Nick said. "And I haven't been using the brace much anymore."

"Well, that's good. Which leg is it?"

"Left."

"Then when it comes to pitching, you got no excuses," Satch said. "Power comes from the back leg. . . . All that front leg does is help you balance at the top and make sure you don't land on your face after you throw." He turned and pointed at the mound. "So get out there and show me your stuff."

Nick slowly walked toward the center of the diamond. The mound was much taller and firmer than the little bump Emma had dug in their backyard, and the divot in the earth where the pitcher's foot landed after he strode forward seemed impossibly far from the rubber—this was a mound for men, not boys. As Nick got into position and took a deep breath, Satch sank into a deep crouch, his bony knees sticking out on either side of the plate like oars on a rowboat.

"Fastball," he shouted. "Right in the glove!"

For a moment Nick was paralyzed by the idea that he was about to throw a ball to Satchel Paige, but then he forced the air from his lungs and focused on the target. His body moved, controlled by instinct, and suddenly all his weight was on his bad leg, his torso perpendicular to the ground, and a sharp snap came from home plate. Satch stood, shaking his hand.

"Lord almighty," he said. "You got a live arm, Hopalong."

Nick wanted to respond, but instead he just smiled like an idiot. Satch tossed the ball back to him. "Ten more," he said. "Just like that."

Nick overthrew the third pitch and bounced it in the dirt, but the rest were good. When Satch caught the last ball, he stood and walked toward the mound. Nick met him on the infield grass.

"You're accurate, too," Satch said. "You practice a lot?"

Nick shrugged. "I drew a target on the wall at the hospital."

"Good. When I was your age, I'd throw rocks at signposts or anything else I could find. Probably a couple hundred a day. That's how you get so you can put the ball wherever you want." Satch paused for a long moment, his dark eyes locked on Nick. "You know, I give folks advice all the time—anything under the sun. But if you held my hand to the Bible, I'd swear that I only know one true thing on this earth. You want to hear it?"

"Of course," Nick said.

"I've got a brother with more talent than me. Arms like a circus strongman and fast as the wind. And, boy, could he throw—he could stand on home plate and toss a ball out of most parks. But when folks told us that we'd never be worth nothing, he listened. And that's why he's living in a shack back home and I'm traveling the world. You understand?"

Nick nodded. He understood exactly what Satch meant and why he was saying it—in fact, his mother used to say a version of the same thing: "There's nothing you can't do if you believe in yourself." When Nick was younger, that had seemed like one of those sweet, bland things that mothers say, but now he wasn't sure whether it was true. You could want to be a major-league pitcher more than anyone else on earth, but if you had a weak arm . . . well, it was going to be pretty close to impossible. But maybe that wasn't Satch's point; maybe he was just saying that you shouldn't let fear get between you and what you want.

Nick was still lost in that thought when Mr. Churchill appeared on the field and waved at Satch. "I'm going over to that meeting now," he called. "You sure you want to come?"

Satch nodded curtly. "I make a point of always negotiating for myself."

"Okay," Mr. Churchill said. He looked at Nick. "Wild Bill thought you were funny, so you're coming too."

"Back to the hotel?" Nick asked.

"Nope," Mr. Churchill said with a flicker of a smile. "Somewhere else."

❊   ❊   ❊

Somewhere else turned out to be the tallest building in North Dakota. The State Capitol, also known as the Skyscraper on the Prairie, towered nineteen floors above Bismarck, and as the elevator whirred upward Nick felt an exhilarating combination of nerves and excitement. The highest he had ever been was either the third floor of the hospital or the time he climbed a giant oak tree near the river.

"How come we're meeting Wild Bill in the Capitol if he's not the governor anymore?" Nick asked as the elevator doors opened onto a hallway on the sixteenth floor.

"Because he still runs this state," Mr. Churchill said, his tone unusually short. "And because he's likely to be governor again as soon as they hold an election."

They pushed their way through a glass door stenciled TOM MILLS, MAJORITY LEADER. A secretary glanced up at them from behind a big desk, and when Mr. Churchill identified himself, she waved them to a small sitting area. Satch put his big feet up on a table and picked his nails as he waited, as calm as if he were sitting on the bench between innings. Mr. Churchill, on the other hand, looked like a slug in the sun. At last the secretary led them into a large room with giant windows. Wild Bill and two other men were sitting in modern-looking chairs, but Nick was mesmerized by the view—beyond the window stretched the tops of roofs and the curl of the Missouri River and the vast expanse of brown fields that eventually faded into the horizon. He was staring down at the nearest street, where the cars looked like toys, when Wild Bill spoke.

"Is that boy Satchel Paige?" he asked. He was ignoring Satch and looking at Mr. Churchill, who just nodded. "What's he doing here?"

"You'll have to ask him," Mr. Churchill said.

Wild Bill turned to Satch, who looked back at him as if he were staring down a batter. "I'm not pitching in that tournament down in Kansas," Satch said after a long moment. "Not unless they put up more than chicken feed for prize money."

Wild Bill wagged a finger at Satch. "Don't get uppity with me," he said. "I promised my friend who runs that tournament that you were going to show up, so you and your team are going to go down there and win one for the state of North Dakota. Like it or not."

"My contract didn't call for no tournaments," Satch said. "If they want me to pitch, I need an appearance fee."

"There is an appearance fee. One thousand dollars. To be split by the team."

Satch shook his head. "We're going to get a thousand dollars for every game we win. To split. Plus an extra thousand dollars to me personally just for showing up."

Wild Bill sputtered for a moment, his face red. "That's highway robbery!"

Satch shrugged. He still looked perfectly calm. "Your friend will still make plenty of money. We'll sell out every game in that brand-new stadium, and he'll get all kinds of free publicity because every newspaper in the country will write a story about how an integrated team from North Dakota somehow managed to win a national tournament."

The room was silent again for almost thirty seconds. Mr. Churchill was shifting uncomfortably on his feet as Satch and Wild Bill stared at each other, the only sound the monotonous ticking from a grandfather clock on the far side of the room.

"I know you're not from around here," Wild Bill finally said. "But ask anyone about me. I run this state and I don't like to be crossed. So I suggest that you and your team get down to that tournament. You understand?"

Another long moment passed and then Satch smiled. "It's real easy," he said. "Your man wants Satch because Satch can fill that new ballpark of his. And if his ballpark is full, he'll make his money. So tell the man to pay me, and I'll put on a show at that tournament that folks will remember for a long time—and fill his pockets while I'm doing it. And if he don't want to pay me . . . well, that's fine. But I don't pitch for favors. Just money."

Satch turned and walked to the door, and as he opened it he glanced over his shoulder. The smile was still on his face.

"I know you're a big man in North Dakota," he said. "But I'm the king of barnstorming baseball. And there ain't nobody who can make the king play if he don't want to play."

opposing dugout, trying to crack their signals. About half the time he would be successful, and the players learned to trust him when he warned them about pitchouts or trick plays. He also was familiar with most of the pitchers from the local teams, and before most games he would be surrounded with Bismarck batters who wanted a scouting report.

After a noontime game on a Saturday—an 8–1 blowout of a traveling team from St. Cloud, Minnesota—Mr. Churchill gathered the team in the center of the diamond.

"I have good news and better news," he said, half shouting to be heard over the clamor of the departing crowd. "The good news is that we've been invited to play in the National Baseball Congress. The better news is that the people who organize the tournament have agreed to pay us a bonus of one thousand dollars for every victory!"

The players stared at one another for a stunned moment and then broke into loud cheers. Mr. Churchill watched them, a satisfied smile on his face, and then waved his hands for silence.

"We leave on Thursday," he said when everyone was quiet. "Same travel plans as usual. And make sure you get some sleep, boys. It's going to take seven wins to take home that trophy."

The team cheered again as Mr. Churchill headed toward the office, and even Nick's father had a smile on his face. They were probably happy about the chance to win a thousand dollars per victory, but Nick mostly was excited that he was going to get to see Satch pitch against teams from all over the country—that was a prize worth more to him than any amount of money.

By the time Nick finished his chores around the ballpark,

CHAPTER FIFTEEN

TOP *of the* EIGHTH

Bismarck won nine of the ten games it played over the next two weeks. Satch continued to pitch brilliantly, and according to Nick's unofficial statistics he now had a 26–2 record with 299 strikeouts and only 14 walks. Sometimes Nick would stare at the numbers and shake his head—it seemed impossible that any pitcher, even one as supernaturally gifted as Satch, could be so consistently dominant. People always talked about his trick pitches or the speed of his fastball, but Nick thought that the secret of his success was his control. When he wanted to hit the inside corner, he hit the inside corner. When he wanted to throw a high fastball, it was perfectly at the numbers. And he did it game after game after game without complaining and without losing his good stuff.

Nick's life at home was also going relatively well because his father seemed to be settling into coaching. At practice he generally worked with the younger pitchers on the team, and during the games he would pace the bench and stare at the

the players were gone. As he walked out the main gate, he was surprised to see Emma sitting on the curb, her glove resting next to her.

"Hey," Nick said. "What are you still doing here?"

"Waiting for you," she said. "My mom wants me to pick up some stuff from the store and I need help getting it home."

"Oh," Nick said. "Okay."

They walked north along a wide street, Nick following Emma's lead. He was still thinking about the tournament when she suddenly paused and pointed into a big park that stretched along the side of the road.

"Aren't those your friends?" she asked.

Nick followed her finger and suddenly realized that she was pointing at the youth baseball field—the place that had practically been his second home before he got sick. A team was taking infield practice, and as Nick focused on them he realized that Emma was right: Tom was at shortstop and Nate was at first.

"Aren't you going to go say hello?" Emma asked.

Nick shrugged. "I don't want to interrupt practice."

Emma looked at him for a long moment and then turned and cupped her hands to her mouth. "Hey," she shouted before Nick could stop her. "You need a pitcher?"

The game paused as every head swung in their direction. Nick wanted to hide behind a tree—or maybe strangle Emma—but it was too late so he slowly walked toward the field, a dull feeling of dread in his stomach. Tom and Nate trotted in from their positions to meet him.

"Are you really ready to pitch again?" Nate asked when he reached the fence.

"I don't know," Nick said.

"I saw him pitch the other day," Emma said. Nick's head swung around—she was standing right behind him. "He looked really good."

"We still need another pitcher," Tom said. "We've got the best hitters in the league, but we give up too many runs."

Nick stared out at the field. While he was trapped in his hospital bed, he had played hundreds of games here in his imagination, and every clump of dirt and kink of the fence felt familiar. A huge part of him craved the feeling of walking back onto the mound—the instant acceptance that would come from being on a team again. But . . .

"My doctor says I can't," Nick finally said. "Sorry."

Nick turned and walked away before anyone could say anything else. Emma hustled to catch him, but she was quiet as they continued toward the center of town. When the five-and-dime store was within sight, Nick glanced at her out of the corner of his eye.

"You knew they were going to be at that park," he said.

She shrugged. "Maybe."

"Why?"

"Because you can pitch," she said in a rush. "It doesn't matter what your dad thinks or whether your leg is perfect or anything else. You *can* pitch and you *want* to pitch. And you won't be happy until you try."

Nick kept walking, silent. It was nice of her to care so much, but Nick also wished she would mind her own business. Nick knew he wasn't ready to play. Yeah, his leg felt a lot better and he could throw off a mound without falling on his face, but what if a batter bunted? Would he be able to sprint forward and grab the ball? Could he run the bases? But those physical fears seemed minor compared to the big one—the feeling of pure terror that Nick got whenever he imagined standing on the mound with everyone watching him and waiting to see if he was a pitcher or a cripple. Nick had been known for one thing before he went to the hospital: being the best young pitcher in Bismarck. And it was petrifying to imagine stepping back onto the field before he really knew whether he was going to ruin that reputation.

While Emma may have had an ulterior motive in asking Nick for help, she hadn't been lying about needing to pick up stuff from the store. Nick ended up walking home with a bag of flour over his shoulder as she lugged two small bags of potatoes. As they rounded the corner of her house, Emma suddenly stopped and pointed at a window. Nick peered inside and saw Emma's mother sitting at the kitchen table. A man was sitting across from her, his back to the window, and as Nick watched, the pair suddenly burst into laughter at some private joke. Something about the way the man threw his head back was oddly familiar—

"Is that my father?" Nick asked, the words bursting from his mouth.

But Emma had dropped the potatoes and was striding away across the yard. Nick leaned the bag of flour against the house and then hurried to catch her. They walked back to the bench behind the house, but instead of sitting she turned on her heel and leaned against a tree. Nick's leg was stiff after the long walk so he settled onto the bench.

"What's the matter?" he asked after a long, silent moment.

Emma stared at him, her face ghostly white in the shadows. "You don't think it's weird?"

"What's weird?"

"Don't play dumb," she said. "First you and your dad came over for dinner, and now they're sitting in the kitchen having a cup of coffee."

Nick thought for a long moment. Yeah, it was weird to see his father laughing with Emma's mother—or anyone else. But life with his father had gotten easier over the past few weeks. He wasn't exactly a chatterbox, but it also didn't sound like he was angry every time he opened his mouth. And maybe Emma's mother had something to do with that or maybe she didn't, but anyone who could make his father laugh was nothing short of a miracle worker.

"I want my dad to be happy," Nick eventually said. "Because maybe if he's happy we'll get to stay in Bismarck. And maybe he won't be so mean."

"Oh," Emma said.

She looked at Nick, something sad in her dark eyes, and she then pushed herself away from the tree and came and sat next to him on the bench. Nick tensed as her head settled onto his shoulder. They were quiet for a long moment. Nick could feel the warmth radiating from her forehead and smell a hint of soap.

"Then I guess it's okay," she finally said. "But I don't want to be your sister. Okay?"

"Okay," Nick said.

CHAPTER SIXTEEN

BOTTOM *of the* EIGHTH

That Thursday the team piled back into the Chrysler and the Plymouth and barnstormed south toward Wichita and the National Baseball Congress World Championship. After a game in Lawrence—just west of Kansas City—Nick and the team walked back to the cars and found a tall, muscular man leaning against the Chrysler, a toothpick between his teeth and a battered suitcase at his feet. Satch broke into a wide smile.

"Are my eyes lying or is that Chet Brewer, the second greatest pitcher on the planet?" he asked nobody in particular.

"Might be," the tall man said. "Although I've heard that Chet Brewer is the best pitcher on this planet or any other planet in the solar system."

Satch glanced at the suitcase. "Are you coming with us to the tournament?"

"Depends." Chet flicked his head at Mr. Churchill. "If he's paying, I'm playing."

"Oh, I'm paying," Mr. Churchill said. "Satch promised me that if we picked you up, we'd go through that tournament like a hot knife through butter."

Satch clapped Mr. Churchill on the shoulder. "I said it and I meant it. Those folks down in Wichita have never seen anything like us."

After three more games in three more days, the team arrived in Wichita—tired yet exhilarated. They were riding a twelve-game winning streak that put their season record at sixty-six wins, fourteen losses, and four ties. Satch had closed his regular season with a typically brilliant stretch, and his final numbers were a 29–2 record with 321 strikeouts and only 16 walks. The numbers proved something Nick already knew—he had witnessed one of the most amazing stretches of pitching in baseball history. Maybe Satch hadn't been facing major-league hitters, but that wasn't his fault; he beat the men he was allowed to play.

The hotels in Wichita were segregated just like in McPherson, but this time Double Duty knew of a few boardinghouses where he and the other black players could sleep and eat. The morning of the first day of the tournament, the team met at registration, which was held in a giant agricultural hall downtown. As they waited in the long, slow-moving line, Nick scanned the program. According to the opening section this was going to be the most diverse tournament ever held in the United States—or maybe anywhere. There were thirty-four teams from twenty-four states, including four all-black teams, a team of Japanese players from California, and an Indian team from Wewoka, Oklahoma. There was even a team made up entirely of men from one family: the ten Stanczak brothers of Illinois.

When the team reached the front of the line, a man popped up from behind the desk, an unnaturally wide smile on his face. He stepped forward and pumped Mr. Churchill's hand.

"Hap Dumont," he said. "I'm the one who put this little shindig together."

"Glad to meet you," Mr. Churchill said. "How do we sign up?"

Hap's smile shrank a few inches. "Well, there are a few men who want to have a little chat with you first."

"What kind of chat?" Mr. Churchill asked.

Hap glanced over his shoulder instead of answering, and three men dressed in suits marched up to the desk. They weren't smiling.

"This is Dan Winters, a member of our board," Hap said, nodding his head at the shortest man. "And the other two gentlemen manage teams in the tournament."

Mr. Churchill glanced at the three men and then looked back at Hap. "Is there a problem?"

"Maybe," Hap said. "These men have raised some objections to the idea of an integrated team playing in the tournament."

"It isn't just us," Dan said. His voice was a low growl. "A lot of people don't think that black folks and white folks should be competing for the same prize."

"That's nonsense," Mr. Churchill said brusquely. "You've got a bunch of black teams and a team filled with Japanese. Why aren't they a problem?"

"Because they aren't integrated," Dan said.

Mr. Churchill folded his arms across his chest and glared

at Hap. "Let me get this straight," he said. "You begged my team to come all the way down here from North Dakota, and now that we show up you say that we can't play?"

"These gentlemen aren't representing my point of view," Hap said. "I want you to play. But they also have rights."

"We might be willing to consider a compromise," one of the other men in suits said. "We'll let everyone on your team play except for him and him and him."

The man's finger moved from Satchel to Double Duty to Chet, who together gave Mr. Churchill a matching set of bemused looks.

"Why not them?" Mr. Churchill asked.

The man opened his mouth to answer, but Satch cut him off. "I'll tell you why," he said. "The man don't object to playing against black folks. He just wants to win and thinks he won't have a chance if we're playing."

"And he's right," Double Duty said quietly.

Nick expected the three men to object, but they just shrugged. "Those boys could play in the big leagues," one of the managers said. "And this is a semipro tournament."

"It ain't my fault that they won't let me play big-league ball," Satch said. "So until they change the rules and the New York Yankees give me a call, I'm semipro. And that's a fact."

Dan ignored him and looked at Hap. "There are several teams that are prepared to pull out of the tournament if they play." He flicked his head at the two men standing beside him. "Including theirs."

Mr. Churchill looked at the third man in a suit, who hadn't said anything yet. "Where are you from?" he asked.

"Fort Smith, Arkansas," the man said in a low drawl.

Mr. Churchill snorted. "If you think anybody in this town is going to shed a tear because they can't watch some team from chicken country, you're crazy." As the man stiffened, Mr. Churchill shifted his gaze to Hap. "You know the drill," he said. "My team will get you the gate because people want to see if my boys are as good as advertised. If the great Satchel Paige really could be a big-league pitcher. That's why you paid us the appearance fee and that's why you're going to keep us in the tournament, even if it means losing a team from the teeming metropolis of Fort Smith, Arkansas."

Everyone stared at Hap—Satch, Mr. Churchill, the rest of the team, and the three fuming men in suits. After a very long moment Hap reached down and pushed a piece of paper across the desk to Mr. Churchill.

"Sign here," he said. "First game is tomorrow."

That game turned out to be against the ten Stanczak brothers, who looked so similar that when they ran onto the field Nick felt like he was watching a funny cartoon. Satch was the starting pitcher, and he gave up two ugly runs in the third on a rare throwing error by Joe Desiderato. The team was losing 3–2 in the seventh and the crowd was buzzing with the possibility of an upset, but Bismarck rallied for four runs and won 6–4.

After the game Nick walked past a thick pack of reporters who were interviewing Julius Stanczak, and he overheard someone ask whether Satch had been throwing hard. Julius's laugh boomed over the sound of flashing bulbs and chatter from the players still on the field. "Throwing hard?" he asked incredulously. "I saw Double Duty put a steak in his glove so

Satch wouldn't take his hand clean off. So, yeah . . . I'd say he was throwing plenty hard."

Chet Brewer started the second game, which was against a team from Missouri, and in the sixth inning he uncharacteristically walked the bases loaded with Bismarck leading by just one run. Satch entered in relief and struck out the side, and the team went on to win 8–4. Games three and four were against the Wichita Watermen—the hometown team— and a team from Shelby, North Carolina. Satch dominated in the first game, aiding his cause by driving in two runs, and Brewer pitched a two-hitter in the second.

The fifth game was against the Duncan Cementers from Oklahoma. They were a brutish team with sluggers up and down the lineup, and to that point in the tournament they had been averaging the stunning total of thirteen runs per game. Mr. Churchill sent Satch to the mound, and he poured cold water on the Cementers' hot bats, striking out sixteen batters in a 3–1 victory. When the team poured into the small locker room beneath the stands after the game, Mr. Churchill clambered onto a chair and cupped his hands to his mouth.

"That's five wins and five thousand dollars!" he shouted to the cheers of the players. "Just two more and we win the whole darned thing!"

Nick watched from the corner, exhilarated yet also drained. He had spent almost every waking hour over the previous two weeks watching baseball—so much, in fact, that for the first time in his life he sometimes found his attention wandering during the late innings of lopsided games. When Bismarck wasn't playing, his father was scouting the other teams, and Nick had spent days perched next to him behind home plate as his father made careful notes in his little moleskin book. They almost never talked. Nick nevertheless liked the feeling of sitting together, and he actually didn't mind the silence. It was easier to enjoy the rhythms of baseball when you were quiet.

Nick was therefore surprised when late in one of the games they were scouting—an error-ridden slugfest between two mediocre teams—his father turned to him.

"The pitcher's tipping," he said gruffly. "Can you spot it?"

Nick was quiet as he watched the next four pitches. He looked for anything unusual—a flare of the glove, a finger pointing toward the sky, a double clutch during the stretch.

"I think he wiggles his shoulders before a curveball," Nick finally said. "Kind of like a shrug."

His father nodded. "Yeah. Do you know why?"

"Maybe he's reminding himself to stay on top of it," Nick said. "Or maybe his shoulder is tight and he's trying to get it loose."

"It's because he doesn't trust his curve," his father said. "But he knows they're sitting fastball so he has to try."

Nick nodded. That made sense. They watched another few pitches in silence, and then Nick glanced at his father out of the corner of his eye.

"Satch told me how he reads batters," he said.

His father kept staring at the pitcher. "Yeah?"

"He says he watches the knee. It tells him if the batter is gearing up for a fastball or keeping his weight back for a breaking pitch."

"I heard that one," his father said. "It's kind of like what I learned from a coach back in prairie ball. You keep your eye on how the batter sets up in the box. If he's trying to take away the curve, he moves as close to the mound as possible. If he's worried that he can't catch the fastball, he's practically sitting in your lap." He paused. "Of course, some batters are smart. They know you're trying to read them, so they mix it up. That's why we scout people. But when you can't scout, you have to use every trick in the book."

Nick was quiet again. He didn't have anything to add, and he didn't want to ruin the moment by saying something stupid. This had been the longest conversation he had shared with his father in years.

CHAPTER SEVENTEEN

TOP *of the* NINTH

The morning of the semifinal game Nick awakened at his usual time and went downstairs to the little restaurant at the hotel to get bread and coffee for Mr. Churchill and his father. He left half the food in his room and then went down the hall and knocked on Mr. Churchill's door. After twenty seconds without a response he knocked again and then pressed his ear against the wood. A moment later he heard what sounded like a faint groan.

"Mr. Churchill," he called. "It's time to get up!"

This time the groan was loud enough to carry clearly into the hall, and Nick tried the door and discovered that it was unlocked. He pushed it open a few inches and then spoke through the crack. "Are you okay, Mr. Churchill?"

"No," Mr. Churchill said, the word trailing off into a long moan. "Get a doctor."

Nick dashed downstairs, moving as quickly as he could on his bad leg—it was always stiff in the morning—and the desk clerk dialed the closest doctor. Ten minutes later a tall man in a dark cloak entered the lobby carrying a black valise. Nick guided him upstairs and then stood in the corner while the doctor conducted his examination to a chorus of labored moans and grunts from Mr. Churchill.

"Your stomach is agitated," the doctor finally said.

"I didn't need a doctor to tell me that," Mr. Churchill said. "I want to know what I can do about it."

"Stay in bed," the doctor said. "And drink lots of water with baking soda."

A moment later he had packed his equipment back into the valise and was gone. Mr. Churchill rolled over in bed, his sheet drawn up over his body like a shroud, and stared at Nick.

"I hate doctors," he said. "Five dollars to give you a bunch of common sense."

"I met some nice doctors," Nick said. "But they want you to do everything they say even though they're sometimes wrong."

Mr. Churchill gave him a pointed look. "Were they wrong about you?"

Nick shrugged, embarrassed. "Maybe."

Mr. Churchill slowly sat up and tried to swing his feet to the floor, but halfway through the motion he hunched over, groaning.

"You're supposed to stay in bed," Nick said.

"I've got to get to the park," Mr. Churchill said. "The team needs a manager."

"If you stay in bed today, maybe you'll get better. You don't want to miss the final, do you?"

Mr. Churchill half smiled and then flopped back against his pillow. "You sound like my mother." He stared at the ceiling for a long moment. "Who's going to manage the team?"

"My dad."

"Your dad is a good man. But I don't know if he's ready to be a manager."

"Sure he is," Nick said. "He was catcher and catchers always make good managers. Plus he knows more about the teams in this tournament than anyone."

"I guess he does," Mr. Churchill said. He rolled over on his side and looked at Nick, his face sallow in the faint light from the window. "Fine. Go tell your father that he's running the show today."

Nick nodded and then let himself out of the room before letting the huge grin spread across his face. His father was shaving in the common bathroom at the end of the hall, and Nick walked up behind him and then paused in the door.

"Mr. Churchill is sick," he said. His father glanced up and looked at Nick in the reflection of the scratched mirror, his eyes dark and unblinking. "He can't manage the team today and wants you to do it."

His father drew the straightedge across the last bit of cream on his cheek and then carefully washed the blade before rinsing his face and patting it dry. When he was finally finished, he turned around to face Nick.

"We're going to win," he said. "Because if we don't, there's no future for us in Bismarck."

The semifinal game was against the Omaha V-8's. Before the first pitch, his father gathered the team and gave them a short scouting report on Omaha's pitchers. Nick could tell

he was nervous by the way he gripped his notebook and the hint of a tremor in his voice.

"It's simple," he said at the conclusion of his scouting report. "Be patient because some of these pitchers can't find the strike zone. And run the moment you get on base because that catcher's got a noodle for an arm. And if we do that, we'll get some early runs and win this one for Mr. Churchill, okay?"

The team nodded quietly in assent and then went out and did exactly what Nick's father had asked. Five of the first nine batters walked, they ran at will on the opposing catcher, and by the time the dust settled they had won 15–6 to advance to the finals. As soon as the game was over, Nick ran back to the hotel with the lineup card. Mr. Churchill was sitting up in his bed, a tall glass of cloudy water perched on his enormous stomach, when Nick burst into his room.

"We won!" Nick said. "We're going to the finals!"

Mr. Churchill punched the air and then looked at Nick, a huge grin on his face. "One more win," he said. "One win and people will remember this team forever."

The championship was a rematch against the Duncan Cementers from Oklahoma. Nick was so nervous that he barely slept the night before the game—maybe Satch had shut them down the first time they played, but it was hard to beat a good team twice. The good news was that the tournament had scheduled a few extra days between the semifinal and final, and Satch therefore would be pitching on a full three days of rest, which was more than he had gotten in months.

The team obviously shared Nick's nerves because the players were quiet as they took pregame batting practice. Even Satch seemed affected; he hopped back and forth on the balls of his feet during the national anthem like a boxer trying to keep warm before a fight. The first few innings of the game were agonizing. Every Cementers hit felt like a punch to Nick's gut—and they had plenty of hits. But Satch was also getting lots of strikeouts, and he managed to limit the damage.

In the top of the seventh it was tied 1–1, and Nick was reduced to huddling at the end of the bench, nervously chewing on his dirty fingernails. Joe Desiderato led off with a double, and Red Haley worked a tough walk before Double Duty hit a soft chopper toward third—an easy out at first, but good enough to advance the runners to second and third. The whole team was standing on their feet and shouting as Moose strode to the plate, but he lunged at the first pitch and hit a soft flare to the shortstop for the second out of the inning. Satch, who had been gently swinging a bat in the on-deck circle, glanced at Mr. Churchill.

"It's good you pay me a lot of money because I've got to do everything myself," he said with a cocky grin.

A moment later he was standing at the plate, his shoulders slumped and his bat twirling a lazy circle over his back shoulder. He looked too sleepy and lanky to be dangerous, but Nick had learned that was just an act. Satch watched the first two pitches—a ball and a strike—his body language betraying no interest in swinging the bat. But as the pitcher went into his windup for the third pitch, Satch crouched, his gaze suddenly intent.

"Come on, Satch!" Nick heard himself yelling. "Hit it!"

Satch had already started his swing, his bat moving forward in a smooth stroke as his head stared down at the ball. A clean *crack* echoed around the ballpark as a white blur streaked past the glove of the leaping second baseman. Nick was on his knees, fist pounding the dirt, as Joe and Red crossed the plate. It was 3–1. They were winning!

"Nine more outs," his father said tersely beside him. "Nine outs to a championship."

Quincy struck out to end the top of the seventh. Nick ran out to bring Satch his glove, but Mr. Churchill got to him first. He was so nervous that the words were pouring out of his mouth in a steady stream.

"How's the arm?" he was asking Satch as Nick approached. "Are you still feeling strong? Should I get Chet up? We've got lots of relief. Hilton can throw too. Or maybe even Double Duty."

Satch put a calming hand on Mr. Churchill's shoulder. "There's no reason to be all crazy," he said. "Why don't you go put your feet up and relax because old Satch has got it from here."

And Satch was exactly right. He gave up nine hits in the game but struck out fourteen, and when the last Cementer swung and missed at a final sharp curveball and the team exploded onto the field in celebration, he just smiled as if the outcome had never been in doubt. He kept that same smile through the awarding of the championship trophy and the special ceremony where the writers covering the tournament gave him the MVP, which was an obvious choice since he'd won four games, gotten a key save, and struck out sixty batters—a record that everyone agreed was likely to stand for a very long time. In fact, his smile didn't fade until the team was back in the little locker room and Quincy Trouppe came over to him and Double Duty and Hilton Smith and Chet Brewer.

"I was just talking to a scout," Quincy said. "And you know what he told me? He said that he would recommend signing all of us to play pro ball for a hundred thousand dollars each if we was white. What do you think about that?"

"I don't want to think about it," Satch said. He glanced at the trophy, which Mr. Churchill was cradling as if it were made out of solid gold. "I just want to enjoy this."

"But that scout was right," Hilton Smith said. "I bet this team would have a good chance of winning a pennant. If they'd just let us play."

"No doubt," Satch said. "And if we had Josh Gibson, we'd win that pennant going away. It wouldn't even be fair." He paused and glanced around the locker room. "I'll tell you one thing and it ain't just talk. . . . I've played on a lot of teams, but this just might be the best."

Satch usually said that kind of stuff like a boast, but this time his voice had a different tone—regret, maybe. And Nick thought he knew why. It was possible that Satch was the best pitcher in the world, yet he never got a real chance to prove it: He should have been facing down the Yankees in the World Series in front of tens of thousands of people rather than dominating a semipro tournament in Kansas. Nick didn't understand why that was fair. Why couldn't Satch and Hilton and Double Duty play in the majors? Who wouldn't want to see the best play against the best? Did the color of a person's skin really matter that much?

It was at moments like these that Nick realized that some things in the adult world simply made no sense. But he was nevertheless grateful for Satch's example—Nick's little limp felt like an awfully minor problem when compared to a rule that prevented you from ever reaching the pinnacle of your profession. Over his few months with the team, Nick had learned many things, but he knew that the most important lesson, the one that would stick with him for the rest of his life, had come from watching the dignified way that Satch dealt with the transparent injustice of his situation.

CHAPTER EIGHTEEN

BOTTOM of the NINTH

Like most barnstorming teams, the Bismarck Churchills fell apart quickly. Hilton Smith and Double Duty left Wichita on a train for points south, and they dropped off Chet Brewer at a gas station on the outskirts of Kansas City. The little caravan of cars pulled back into Bismarck late on a Monday afternoon, and by the time Nick finished unloading the gear, most of the remaining players were already gone. For a terrible moment Nick thought he had missed his chance to say good-bye to Satch, but then the familiar convertible pulled up next to the Plymouth.

"So long, Hopalong," Satch said as he rolled down his window. He glanced at Nick's legs. "Although I got to admit that nickname doesn't seem right, now that you don't have much of a hitch in your gait."

"It's okay," Nick said. "I kind of like it." He paused. "Are you coming back next season?"

Satch shook his head. "I've learned never to say never.

But I think old Satch has worn out his welcome here in Bismarck."

Nick was going to ask why he had worn out his welcome, but Mr. Churchill had wandered over from the office. He stuck out his hand, which Satch shook.

"You did what you promised," Mr. Churchill said. "And I sure am grateful."

Satch smiled a salesman's grin. "I always do what I promise." The smile dimmed. "So what kind of deal did you cut with Wild Bill? Did he promise you something if we won the tournament?"

"A gentleman never tells," Mr. Churchill said. "But don't be surprised if someday I end up being the mayor of this little town."

Satch raised an eyebrow. "If you send me the keys to the city, maybe I'll come back."

"Okay," Mr. Churchill said. "Deal."

They shook hands again, and then Mr. Churchill walked toward his office. He paused in the doorway and glanced back at the convertible. "You can forget the rest of the payments on that car," he said loudly.

Satch winked. "That's good. Because I wasn't going to pay you anyhow."

Mr. Churchill snorted and then disappeared into the office. Satch looked at Nick and then reached into a bag sitting on the passenger seat and pulled out a glass bottle filled with a familiar liquid—deer oil.

"I got this for you," he said. "I know your leg is feeling better, so maybe you can use it on your arm. Once you start pitching again."

Nick carefully took the bottle. "Thanks, Satch."

Satch turned the key, and the convertible's engine started with a sputter. The car lurched into gear and drove a few feet forward, but then it stopped. Satch glanced over his shoulder.

"Hey, Hopalong," he said. "Here's one more piece of old Satch's famous wisdom. . . . Don't look back. Something might be gaining on you."

Satch waved a giant hand and then the tires spun and he was gone. Nick stood frozen amid the swirling dust, wondering what he was supposed to do now. All summer the team had been his life, but now with one roar of an engine it was over—the Bismarck Churchills would be a team in name only until the following spring. In fact, Nick didn't even know if he and his father would be back the following season. Maybe they would move to a new town or maybe his father would become a manager on a different team or give up baseball or . . .

Nick's head swirled; it was all just too overwhelming. He had gotten used to the faces on the team: Satch and Quincy and Barney and Hilton and Joe and Double Duty and Red and Moose and Chet. They had been his family—and a way to avoid the reality of his return from the hospital—but that was over now. It was time for him to make his own life, which meant that he had to stop hiding. The challenge was finding a way to start.

It began, of course, with baseball. The day after the team returned from the tournament, Nick was pumping water in the yard when Emma emerged from her house.

"That team wants you to play," she said. "Another one of their pitchers got hurt and they need help. Today."

"The team with Tom and Nate?" Nick asked, stalling for time.

"Of course," she said. "I told them you had been practicing and could pitch at least a couple of innings."

Nick could feel the familiar fear rising in his chest, but he knew this was an important moment. It wasn't going to get any easier to throw himself back into his old life.

"Okay," he said before he could change his mind. "Just let me get my glove. And tell my father."

"He's in my house," Emma said, an eyebrow raised. "Fixing the stove."

Nick just grunted and then went and got his glove from the cabin. He changed his mind ten times about whether he actually would tell his father, but when he got back to the yard, he walked straight past Emma and into the main house. He followed the sound of their voices to the kitchen, where his father was patching a rusty spot on the stove's iron chimney as Mrs. Landry watched from the kitchen table. They were in the middle of a conversation, a smile on both their faces, but they stopped abruptly as Nick came through the swinging door.

"I'm going to play baseball," Nick said, his eyes locked on his father. "A team wants me to pitch." His father just stared at him, expressionless. "And I haven't been wearing my brace. Not for weeks."

"I know," his father said. "I decided that if you're determined to be a fool, I'm not going to stop you."

Nick felt his cheeks flush, and the words came in a

jumble: "My leg's doing better. It's not perfect, but that's okay. I mean, nothing is perfect, right? Because if things were perfect Mom would still be here and you would still be playing baseball and wouldn't say mean things all the time."

His father was silent for what felt like a minute, and then he picked up his sandpaper and returned to working on the chimney. Nick watched him for a few ferocious strokes and then turned and headed for the door.

"Don't raise your voice at me," his father said as the door swung shut. "Ever again."

Nick ignored him and went outside. Emma was still waiting in the yard, and when she noticed the expression on his face, she instinctively touched his arm.

"What is it?" she asked. "Are you okay?"

"I'm fine," Nick said.

"What were they doing?"

"Just talking." Nick paused. "I think they're friends. Which is good, I guess. My dad doesn't have any friends. Just teammates."

"What about you?" Emma asked. "Do you have friends?"

Her dark eyes were locked on him, and Nick tried to shrug nonchalantly. "Well, there's this one girl. She's done a lot of really nice things for me, and I feel bad because I haven't really thanked her."

"Tell me more about this girl," Emma said with a hint of a smile. "She sounds nice."

"It's just someone from the neighborhood. She knows a little bit about baseball. I mean, for a girl."

Emma's smile grew and she stared at him for another long

moment. "I like it when you make jokes," she finally said. "You're usually so serious."

"I used to joke a lot," Nick said. "But it felt kind of weird to laugh in the hospital, so I guess I just kind of got out of the habit." He paused, suddenly nervous. "I got something for you. You know, to say thanks for stuff."

Nick quickly walked back into his cabin, feeling Emma's eyes on him the whole way. He retrieved the little packet from under his bed, and when he got back outside, he hid it behind his back until he was again at her side.

"What is it?" she asked, trying to see around his body.

Nick twisted away, teasing her for one more second, and then pulled the packet from behind his back and handed it to her. "Programs," he said. "One from every game this season. I got the players to sign most of them too. . . . Satch, Hilton Smith, Double Duty, Red. Even Mr. Churchill."

Emma stared at the packet for a long moment, her face even whiter than usual, and the next thing Nick knew her arms were around his neck. He hugged her back, enjoying the moment, but also feeling a little awkward—the last time he'd hugged anyone it had been his mother. When they separated, Nick instinctively adjusted his shirt. She was staring at him, the small smile back on her face—but this time it wasn't because of a joke. Nick glanced down at his feet, suddenly embarrassed.

"You want to come to the game?" he asked.

"I wouldn't miss it for the world," she said.

The first part was easy. Nick's adrenaline was surging as he walked up to the team, and it felt like old times as he met the other players, put on a uniform, and talked to the coach. But as soon as he sat on the bench at the beginning of the game, all of that energy leaked out of his body and suddenly Nick was as nervous as he had ever been in his life. Just because you decided that you ought to be ready to do something didn't mean you were actually ready, and Nick wished he had been practicing more. And why hadn't he insisted on throwing a batting practice or something before appearing in an actual game? Was he crazy?

Nick therefore focused on praying that the team wouldn't actually have to use him, but they were tearing through pitchers, and in the bottom of the fifth the coach turned to him and said, "You're next." Nick remained frozen on the bench for a few seconds and then forced himself to stand and start pinwheeling his arm the way his father had taught him. He glanced at the team, wondering if anyone would be willing to warm him up, but the other kids were all focused on the field. Just as Nick decided that he should ask Emma, someone tapped on his shoulder. It was his father. He was holding his catcher's mitt in one hand.

"You're not going to be any good if you don't get loose," he said.

Nick stared at him for a stunned moment. "Okay," he finally said.

They went to the little warm-up mound beside the field, and his father lowered himself into a crouch. Nick threw ten pitches, starting slowly before gradually building to his best fastball. His father didn't say a word until they were walking back to the dugout.

"Have you been practicing a breaking pitch?" he asked.

"No," Nick said.

"Then don't throw one. You won't be able to control it, and you'll just hurt your arm. Stick with the fastball, low. Work both sides of the plate."

Nick just nodded. He expected his father to walk off the field, but instead he stopped, his hand awkwardly gripping Nick's shoulder.

"I know things haven't been easy for us since your ma passed," he said. "But Mr. Churchill says that you did a good job for him this season and that you can work for him anytime. Which is a good offer because he's a big man around here."

Nick knew what his father really meant, and he was grateful. Maybe it would be easier if his father could just say what he felt—if he could tell Nick that he was proud of him or even just that he was glad he was back from the hospital—but Nick had learned over the past few years to enjoy the good moments in life because things were never going to be perfect.

"I miss her too," Nick finally said.

His father was frozen for a moment, his eyes wide and unblinking. "I know," he said.

He turned and quickly walked off the field. Nick watched him go and then glanced at the bench—just in time to realize that the coach was pointing at him.

"You're up," he said. "Throw strikes and let your defense do the work."

Nick slowly walked onto the field, feeling like every pair of eyes was locked on him, but when he reached the mound, his instincts took over. He stubbed his toe into the rubber to make sure it was firmly planted into the ground and then waited for the catcher to get into position so he could throw his five warm-up tosses. The final one made a satisfying crack in the mitt, and as the catcher threw down to second, Tom jogged in from his position at shortstop.

"It's good to have you back," he said. "Go get 'em."

Nick nodded and stepped back onto the rubber. He took a moment before he looked in for the sign to glance around the field. His father was still behind the bench, one hand gripping the chain-link fence like a claw. Emma was up on the small hill behind home plate, and when she noticed his gaze, she waved. Nick took a deep breath, just the way his father had taught him, and as he exhaled and began his windup, one final thought flashed through his head.

He was home.

HISTORICAL NOTES

I have done my best to be accurate, but many details from this season exist only in legend. One fact is indisputably wrong—Satchel Paige did face a young Joe DiMaggio, but it was in February of 1936. The cable from the Yankee scout who saw the game read: "DiMaggio all we hoped he'd be. Hit Satch one for four."

In 1936, the year following this story, the National Baseball Congress refused to allow any integrated or all-black teams to play in its tournament. Neil Churchill served as the mayor of Bismarck from 1939 to 1946 and was prominent in the community until his death in 1969.

Satchel Paige's dream of playing in the major leagues was realized on July 9, 1948, when he came into a game between the St. Louis Browns and the Cleveland Indians as a relief pitcher. Over the remainder of that season he compiled a 6–1 record with a stellar 2.48 ERA and two shutouts. He was forty-two years old.